Just My Luck

ADAPTED BY LAURIE CALKHOVEN
STORY BY JONATHAN BERNSTEIN AND
MARK BLACKWELL AND JAMES GREER
AND I. MARLENE KING
SCREENPLAY BY I. MARLENE KING AND
AMY B. HARRIS

SCHOLASTIC INC.
New York   London   Toronto   Auckland   Sydney
Mexico City   Hong Kong   New Delhi   Buenos Aires

ISBN 0-439-83137-7

Published by Scholastic Inc.
SCHOLASTIC and associated logos are trademarks and/or registered trademarks
of Scholastic Inc.

12 11 10 9 8 7 6 5 4 3 2 1   6 7 8 9 10/0

Designed by Angela Jun
Printed in the U.S.A.
First printing, February 2006

Prologue

The emergency room nurse yawned and listened to the radio. A bored cleaning woman mopped the floor.

"Up next, we've got a world premiere," the radio DJ said. "Remember where you were when you heard this song, because your life may never be the same. Take it away, Madonna!"

Madonna's voice rang out, *"You must be my lucky star . . ."*

The emergency room doors slammed open. A pregnant woman screamed. A doctor ran on one side of her stretcher and an ambulance attendant on the other.

"She's about to give birth!" the ambulance driver shouted.

"Hold on!" yelled the doctor.

The woman screamed again. The stretcher pounded through another set of doors marked LABOR ROOM SEVEN.

A hospital administrator rushed in carrying a giant gift basket with a balloon welcoming St. Genevieve Hospital's ten-thousandth baby. His assistant carried a huge check, made out to the baby's college fund.

The woman howled. There was a slap. Then a baby's cry.

No one noticed two shooting stars fire across the sky, crossing each other's paths. For a fleeting moment, their sparkling trails left a giant X in the dark night sky.

✳ Chapter One

21 Years and 7 Months Later

"Morning, Oscar," Ashley Albright said to her doorman as she glided out of her Manhattan high-rise. She stood under the building's awning, safe from the rain that poured down around her.

Oscar blew his whistle. "Morning, Miss Albright. Finding a cab may take a while in this mess. No umbrella?"

"You think I'll really need one?" As Ashley finished her sentence, the rain stopped.

Oscar checked the sky. "Guess not," he said. A taxi pulled to a stop in front of him.

Smart, beautiful, and very, very lucky Ashley Albright flashed Oscar a big smile as he held open the taxi door. "Thanks, Oscar."

As she stepped into the cab, she noticed something stuck to the bottom of her stylish shoe. "Sweet!" She slid the five-dollar bill into her pocket.

"First stop, Sixty-sixth and Broadway. I need to be there in" — Ashley checked her watch — "four minutes."

The driver rolled his eyes. "Oh, yeah," he laughed. "Like that's gonna happen." He turned up the radio and pulled into traffic.

Ashley dialed her cell phone. "Hello?"

"WROK Morning Zoo!" said the voice on the other end. "You're caller number thirteen. Can you name our mystery song?"

"Oops, I did it again," Ashley said. "Sorry."

"That's right," said the voice on the phone. "You win —"

Ashley hung up and dialed again.

The taxi driver zipped through a green light and winked at the Yoda bobble-head doll on his dashboard. "Mmmm," he said in a Yoda voice. "Five greens in a row. The Force is strong this morning."

Ashley ignored him. "Hello, Dana?" she said into her phone. "I'm going to be early, so I'm stopping by Balducci's. Muffin?"

The taxi barreled through an intersection, hitting a huge puddle. Water flew in all directions, totally soaking a guy sitting in a bus shelter. Ashley was too busy talking on the phone to notice.

Jake Harden spit the gutter water out of his mouth and looked down at his grungy and now drenched clothes. He pulled a towel out of his backpack and patted his dripping face.

Instead of looking up the avenue for the bus, he kept his eyes trained on the entrance to the super-chic, superexpensive apartment building across the street. A limo waited out front.

Checking the sky for rain, his eyes swept back to the building across the street, and then to the sidewalk in front of him. He spotted a shiny penny, heads up. Glancing around to see if anyone else had noticed it, Jake reached for the penny.

Rip.

He looked at the coin, knowing his pants had just split. "Yup," he groaned. "Canadian."

He was rooting through his backpack for a safety pin when the doorman across the street rushed to open the door for a hip, classy African-American man.

Damon Phillips and his little dog were on the move.

Phillips waved off his chauffeur and headed

toward Central Park, while Jake pricked his finger with his safety pin.

Jake grabbed a CD from his backpack. "No guts, no glory," he muttered and set off at a run.

Phillips strolled through the park. He thought about leaving his dog's poop in the middle of the path for someone else to clean up, but a police officer stood nearby. The only paper Phillips had to use as a pooper-scooper was a five-dollar bill.

A moment later, Jake came to the same fork in the path. He saw the five-dollar bill in the trash can. No one else was watching, so Jake grabbed it and shoved it into his pocket.

"Arrrrghhhhh!" he yelled, when he realized what was in his hand, and knelt at a puddle to wash.

A beautiful jogger rounded the Boat Pond. She looked over her shoulder to smile at Phillips and his dog, and slammed right into Jake, sending him into the puddle.

Jake tried to help her up.

"Get your hands off me!" she screamed.

"I was just —" Jake stood.

Whomp.

The jogger punched Jake in the stomach, screaming for help.

"No. No." Jake held up his hands. "I was just . . ."

"You!" The police officer ran toward Jake. "Stay right there!"

"Uh-oh," Jake said. "This is not good. Definitely not good." He took off after Phillips, running as fast as he could.

Phillips didn't notice. He pressed the speed dial on his cell phone. "I'm ready. The Seventy-first Street entrance to the park. In ten seconds."

The limo skidded to a stop directly in front of Phillips nine seconds later as he emerged from Central Park.

Jake saw his last chance. "Wait," he yelled, hurtling toward the car.

But suddenly Jake was tackled from behind. The CD flew out of his hand and skidded across the asphalt, landing under the limo's tire.

Crunch.

The cop twisted Jake's arm behind his back while Phillips's limo rolled away. Beck's song "Loser" drifted out of the window. *"I'm a loser, baby . . ."*

Jake, handcuffed, banged his head on the ground.

✳ Chapter Two

Ashley strolled into her office building, swinging her Balducci's bag and refreshing her lipstick. Just when she needed it, two men walked past with a large mirror. Hair and makeup perfect, she smiled at her reflection and headed for a crowded elevator. The doors closed in her face.

"Huh?" she said, baffled.

Ding.

"Oh." Ashley nodded as another elevator opened. "I get it." She pressed the button for her floor. The doors started to close.

"Hold it!" someone yelled.

Ashley pushed her arm into the opening. In bounced an extreme hottie, wearing Ashley's favorite designer — Armani.

"Thanks." He grinned.

Ashley grinned back.

Soon they were laughing, then flirting, and then they were making a date.

The doors opened on Ashley's floor.

"Promise? Six o'clock?" the hottie asked.

Ashley stepped off the elevator with a smile. "Okay, David. I'll be the cute redhead who looks like this." She struck a pose.

"In that case," David said, "I'll be there at five thirty."

Ashley walked down the hall with a smile on her face, not noticing the alarm sounding behind her. The elevator she missed had gotten stuck. The doors opened a few inches and then slammed shut, over and over again. A crowd of people was trapped inside.

Breezing through glass doors that read BRADEN & COMPANY PUBLIC RELATIONS, Ashley collected her phone messages from the receptionist.

"Morning, Maggie," Ashley sang to her oldest and best friend. The cute blond was delivering mail and rocking to the beat coming from her headphones.

"What are you so chipper about?" Maggie asked.

"Brad Pitt and Jude Law had a baby, and I just met him in the elevator," Ashley said.

They wended their way through a small sea of cubicles and bumped into Maggie's roommate.

"What's up?" Dana did a double take at Ashley's coat. "Is that a new coat?"

"Can you believe it?" Ashley twirled. "Sample sale. Eighty percent off!"

"And her coat met someone," Maggie added.

Ashley held out David's business card.

"David Pennington," Dana read. "Owner of the Boston Celtics, David Pennington?"

"Gross! Of course not." Ashley batted her eyelashes. "His son." She plopped down in her cubicle and passed out the Balducci's muffins while Dana handed her a Starbucks' latte.

"Impressive," Dana said. "But I, too, had a great morning. Apparently Saturn is in line with Neptune. You know what that means?"

Ashley and Maggie gave her blank stares.

"I have so-so job prospects and my chance for love is on the wane."

"Dana," Ashley said. "You know those things aren't exactly factual."

Maggie's morning wasn't so great either. "And my new song got a really polite rejection letter from Two Tone records. But you know what they say," she added. "When one door closes, two others open."

"That's true!" Ashley said. She glanced at her clock. Eight fifty-eight. "Uh-oh! I have to take the notes for the Phillips meeting. See you later, guys."

She grabbed her laptop and some papers and headed down the hall. She didn't notice the maintenance crew trying to pry open the stuck elevator, while the people inside shouted to be let out.

Ashley set up her laptop in an empty conference room. A trio of hip, black-suited young men rushed in, surrounding Damon Phillips.

Phillips, President of Downtown Masquerade Records, stared at the empty room. "I thought we had a meeting," he said.

"They'll be here soon," Ashley said. "If you care to —"

"Wait?" asked one of Phillips's followers. "This is an insult! D doesn't wait — for anyone."

"That's right," said another of the young men. "For no one. He is furious."

"It's true," Phillips said with a blank expression. "I am furious."

"I'm sure they'll be here any second," Ashley stammered. She tapped her keyboard and made sure they couldn't see the screen. "Oh, look!" she lied, looking at the photo of herself, Maggie, and

Dana at a Halloween costume party. "I just got an instant message. Ms. Braden is putting some final touches on an extra-special presentation for you and she'll be right here."

Phillips stopped keying his BlackBerry. "Do you know how much money Downtown Masquerade Records made last year?"

"Yes. Five hundred and seven million dollars," Ashley answered. "Gross."

"Very impressive! You really know your stuff. Therefore you must know that each *minute* of my time is worth —"

Phillips's follower punched buttons on a calculator. "Nine hundred and sixty-four dollars," he shouted.

"Wow!" Even Phillips was surprised. "That's a lot of money. I did not expect that."

"And that includes the time you're sleeping," said one of the followers.

"So now you see why I have no time to waste. And this" — Phillips waved his arm around the empty conference room — "is wasted time." He got up to leave.

Ashley jumped to her feet. "I completely get that. If you could just give me a moment . . . I'll start."

Phillips shook his head and headed for the door.

"Please," Ashley said. "If it's not worth the minute, I'll give you nine hundred and sixty-five dollars. Because, personally, I think you're underpaid."

Phillips smiled. "You've got guts. Continue."

Ashley gulped. She stared at her laptop screen and saw the picture of herself and her best friends partying on Halloween. "I could talk to you about branding," she said, "but you may want to consider . . ."

✳ Chapter Three

Maggie stopped pushing her mail cart long enough to watch Ashley, Phillips, and his minions leave the conference room.

Just then, the maintenance crew finally got the elevator doors open. Peggy Braden, Ashley's boss, pushed them out of her way and rushed toward Phillips, her staff in tow.

"Damon," she said, looking sophisticated and tough in her black suit. "I'm so sorry we kept you waiting. We'll get our files and start our presentation —"

"No need," he interrupted. "We're done."

"But Damon, please," she pleaded. "The elevator."

"Miss Albright pitched me your entire public relations strategy. I am . . ."

Peggy held her breath.

"Ecstatic," Phillips said.

"Oh?"

"Especially about the party," Phillips added.

"Party?" Peggy asked, trying to hide her confusion.

"Yes, that whole Masquerade Bash. Great idea."

"Oh, you liked that?" Peggy signaled Ashley with her eyes.

"It's a great way to showcase our artists, support a worthy cause, and get a write-off. And, you know me" — Phillips patted his chest — "I never say no to a party."

"Me either," Peggy said, trying to be cool. "I love to par-tay!" Her long earrings jangled, but her blond updo didn't move.

Phillips raised his eyebrows. *Par-tay?* He smiled awkwardly and swept out with his followers.

As soon as he was out of hearing range, Peggy turned to Ashley. "Masquerade Bash?"

"I'm so sorry, Ms. Braden. I took notes at the other meetings. The rest, I improvised." Ashley smiled weakly. Would Ms. Braden be mad?

Peggy took a deep breath. "Well," she said slowly, "it looks like we've got a party to plan."

"Right. Right." Ashley waited.

"You'll need an office."

"Me? An office?" Ashley asked.

"The first rule of business — delegate responsibility," Peggy answered. "That way I can hand out blame — or take the credit. Your idea. You're in charge."

Peggy turned to an assistant. "Find her an office. And get her a company credit card."

Ashley's voice rose with excitement. "Credit card! Thank you, Ms. Braden. Thank you!"

"Ashley, please. From now on, it's Peggy."

"Okay," Ashley answered with a huge smile. "Peggy."

Peggy swept down the hall, passing Maggie, who pretended not to be listening.

"Who are you?" Peggy barked.

"Mail room —"

"Whatever." Peggy turned on her heel and locked eyes with Ashley again. "And don't worry, Ashley. I'll be watching your every move."

Jake trudged down the front stairs of the police station, putting on his backpack. Just as he reached the sidewalk, it started to pour again. Within seconds he was drenched.

✳ Chapter Four

Ashley unpacked her files in a cool new office. Dana crashed on the couch, her feet propped on Maggie's cart, while Maggie took in the amazing view.

"This office is bigger than Dana's and my apartment," Maggie said. "And definitely cleaner."

Dana pointed at Ashley. "As *luck* would have it."

"Would you stop with all that *luck* stuff," Ashley said. "I've worked hard and paid my dues for this promotion."

"Right," Dana answered. "What's it been, six whole months since you dropped out of college? You deserve this."

"Dana, good things happen to Ashley because she puts a positive energy out into the world."

"Thank you, Maggie," Ashley said.

"I send out positive energy!" Dana threw a pillow at Maggie. "Where's my new office? Where's my hunky date?"

"Hey," Ashley said with a laugh. "I flirted like crazy in that elevator. I *earned* that date."

Twenty blocks away, Jake's run-down tenement apartment building, on a block filled with other tenement apartment buildings, looked like it belonged in a different city from Ashley's high-rise.

He left his apartment, his clothes dried and repaired, stopping to buzz the intercom.

"Katy?"

A second later, Katy responded. "Hey, Jake."

"Burger or tuna melt," he said into the intercom.

"Burger, please."

"You got it. See you later," Jake said.

Jake stepped onto the sidewalk. A glob of pigeon poop hit his shoulder. He shook his head and trudged across the street to the Rock 'n' Bowl. Music wafted out.

Walking past the bowling lanes, Jake stopped to listen to a young British band, McFly, do a sound check.

Tom, the young, grungy, and totally talented lead singer, spotted him. "How'd it go?" he asked.

Jake gave him a thumbs-up.

"So you got Phillips the CD?" Tom asked.

"Not yet. We had some scheduling conflicts."

Harry, the drummer, threw down his sticks. "This has been going on for weeks, Jake."

"It's okay," Jake answered. "Remember *'It's a long way to the top if you wanna rock 'n' roll.'*"

"You're quoting AC/DC to us?" asked Danny, McFly's guitar player.

"Is that a problem?" Jake asked.

"Not at all," Danny said sarcastically. "Thank you for the reality check."

"Look, we are on the right track. There are even going to be a couple of A&R guys here tonight." Jake turned to Tom. "So, Tom, even if you really feel it in the moment, don't take off your pants and throw them at the audience."

"But trouser-throwing is Tom's thing," Danny said.

"And it's an awesome, awesome thing." Jake zeroed in on Tom. "Don't do it."

Mac, the owner of the Rock 'n' Bowl, shuffled over. "Hey, Jake. There's a clogged toilet in the men's room."

Jake looked away, embarrassed to talk about

toilets in front of the band. "Looking forward to plunging it, Mac," he hissed. "But not until my shift starts, which is in . . . two hours."

Mac handed Jake the plunger. "Do it now. Pretend it's a Grammy."

✳ Chapter Five

Ashley, hair up and makeup finished, tossed another dress onto her bed. Clothes were everywhere, but Ashley was still in her underwear. Nothing seemed quite right. She vetoed in quick succession a black Heidi Sherman pantsuit, a silky green lace tank top, a multicolored strapless dress, a pink skirt, and a green-and-white sequined top.

She held the minidress up in front of her.

"Too skimpy," said Maggie.

"Where's he taking you?" asked Dana.

"To a basketball game. His dad's team is playing Philly." Ashley tried another outfit.

"Not skimpy enough," joked Dana. "Where's the game — home or away?"

"Away."

"Let me guess. You'll go there on his private jet. Which he flies himself," Dana said.

"You're soooo wrong. He has a pilot." Ashley held up a third, very skimpy outfit.

"Is that even technically clothing?" Maggie teased.

Ashley threw the dress at Maggie and went back to her closet.

"Speaking of dates," Dana said. "We should try to find the Dragon Lady one for the Masquerade Bash. That way she won't be watching our every move."

"Good luck," Ashley said. "Men of Peggy's caliber don't exactly take ads in the yellow pages."

Maggie rolled her eyes. "Could you possibly idolize her a little more?"

"What?" Ashley said. "She's sophisticated, glamorous, gets invited everywhere, and *never* has to stay home because she doesn't have anything to wear."

The doorbell rang.

"Coming," Ashley yelled.

Dana raced her to the door and spied through the peephole. An extremely cute guy in a tuxedo waited outside.

"Whoa!" she whispered. "Who's that? Give me one of those skimpy outfits."

Ashley peeked through the hole. "Down, girl. You're drooling. It's just my next-door neighbor."

Ashley, still in her underwear, opened the door a crack. "Antonio?"

Dana and Maggie shared a look and mouthed, "Antonio."

"Hey, Ashley. Your dry cleaning got delivered while you were out, so I took it."

"As if by *magic*," Dana said under her breath.

Ashley shot Dana a look and turned back to her neighbor. "Thanks, Antonio. You're an angel."

"I do what I can," he said, handing her the dry cleaning. "Big date tonight?"

Ashley nodded. "Kind of big. You?"

"*Every* night is a big date night for me," he said. "You have fun."

Antonio was halfway down the hall when Ashley got an idea. "Hey, Antonio." She poked her head out the door. "Are you free next Thursday?"

"I'm never free." Antonio stopped. "What did you have in mind?"

"This is something you won't want to miss. Masquerade is having an outrageous party. Food, fun, dancing, and . . ." She paused for effect. "A blind date — with my boss."

"What's she like?" Antonio asked.

"A very strong woman, independent, smart —"

"Ashley in ten years," Maggie shouted.

"Good-looking?" Antonio asked.

"Of course," Ashley said.

"Sounds hot. Look, if you think we'll hit it off, that's good enough for me."

"You're the best," Ashley called out before shutting the door. "Yes!" she said, leaning against it. "A date for the Dragon Lady."

She checked out the dry-cleaning bag and her face fell. "These aren't mine." She searched for the tag. "This is Sarah Jessica Parker's!"

Maggie's jaw dropped. "I didn't know she lived in your building."

Dana checked out the designer clothes. "Look! Dolce!"

"I'll bring it back to her tomorrow," Ashley said, her eyes lingering on the designer duds.

"They're just your size," Dana said sarcastically. "What are the odds?"

Ashley eyed Maggie, who nodded. "Why not?" she said.

"You know," Ashley said slowly. "This might actually be cute on me."

Dana rubbed her temples. "I need some chocolate."

*Chapter Six

Jake trudged up the five flights of stairs to his apartment, knocking on the door of apartment number twelve.

"Katy. I'm home!"

Ten-year-old Katy opened the door to her tiny apartment, blowing a huge bubble. She was layered in five or six sweaters. There was a little toy soldier stuck to her face.

"What happened to you?" Jake asked.

"Fourth-grade boys," Katy announced with her Bronx accent.

"What's it stuck on there with?"

"Krazy Glue."

"Ouch," Jake said. "But I bet you had a better day than me."

"That's why you're my boy, Jake," Katy said.

"It's chilly in here."

"Sweaters are free. The heat's not," she said.

Jake handed her one of his bags.

"Burger?" she asked.

"Ketchup for you," Jake said.

Katy's grandma crossed the small living room in her waitress uniform.

"Hi, Jake," she said.

"Hey, Mrs. Martin."

"Katy, I'll be home after my shift — around midnight. Stay out of trouble."

"Okay, Grandma."

Jake searched through his backpack for nail polish remover. "Didn't she just come back from a shift?"

"Double shift today," Katy said.

Jake's face fell for a second. Katy's life was harder than it should be. "Get your face over here," he said.

"Is it going to sting? Because I like wearing it."

"Not if you hold still." Jake worked on removing the toy without hurting Katy's cheek. "Homework?"

"The dog ate it," Katy said.

Jake looked at her.

"Really — they had to pump his stomach and everything."

"Come over later and I'll help you redo it," Jake said.

Katy rubbed her toy-free cheek and smiled.

"What do you say?"

"Thank you, Jake." Katy pretended to swoon. "You're my hero."

Jake shook his head and headed for his own apartment. The number thirteen had been hacked off the door and replaced with a horseshoe — points facing up to hold good luck inside — and a Lucky Charms leprechaun. He unlocked the door to an apartment even smaller than Katy's. As he closed the door behind him the horseshoe jiggled loose. Its points faced down.

The chauffeur opened the door to the stretch limo. Ashley, looking stunning in Sarah Jessica Parker's Dolce, stepped out onto a red carpet, followed by David. A private helicopter waited.

"I thought we were taking a jet?" Ashley said.

"This takes us *to* the jet," David answered.

"Okay. This is definitely going in my diary." Ashley laughed and climbed on board.

They took off with a view of the glorious Manhattan skyline.

✳ Chapter Seven

Jake stood in a thick tangle of cords behind the soundboard and checked out the crowd. It was small, but enthusiastic. He dimmed the lights and grabbed the microphone.

"Give it up for . . . McFly!"

The band struck their first chord.

Jake bent down to adjust the sound, and his jeans slipped down around his hips. He hiked them up, popping the safety pin and pricking his finger. In pain, he whipped his hand back, only to yank out a bunch of cords.

The band played. But no sound came out of the speakers.

"What the . . . ?" Jake bent down and frantically plugged cords back in as McFly's sound came in and out, in and out. Dougie, the bass player, played weird Japanese pop music one minute and high-pitched screeches the next.

The band stared daggers at Jake while the crowd hooted and hollered at him to fix the sound.

"You're firing me?" Jake said later, as he switched off the lights on the bowling lanes. "You don't even *pay* me."

"Look, you're good," Harry said. "I mean, you found us."

"But? What's the but?" Jake prodded.

"But we think it might be time to go back home," Tom answered.

"No, you can't —"

"Jake, we haven't had one lucky break. Besides, my dad needs me back home at the shop in England."

"And Dougie misses his mum," Danny teased.

"Shut it," Dougie warned.

"It's true," Danny said. "He cries every night."

Dougie slugged Danny in the shoulder.

Jake tried to get everyone to listen. "Guys, look. You're so talented. Give me a week. If I can't make something happen for McFly by then, I get it. We're done. Just give me one more week."

The band exchanged glances.

Tom turned to Jake. "One week."

Ashley, Dana, and Maggie talked about her date with David at their favorite sushi restaurant.

"So how was it?" Dana asked.

"It was a first date," Ashley said.

"And I repeat. How was it?"

"It was nice."

"Nice?" Dana persisted. "Did you kiss him?"

"David Pennington is a gentleman," Ashley answered with a dreamy smile.

Maggie wanted to know even more. "Was it a normal kiss or some kind of supernatural, tingling-in-your-toes, butterflies-in-your-stomach kind of kiss?"

"Check, please, Zuki," Ashley said to the waiter, then turned back to her friends. "I'll only say that he asked for another date."

Ashley grabbed the check and whipped out her new company credit card. She held it up to her ear. "What's that? Sí, Señor Platinum. Gracias."

She waved the card in the air and dropped it on the tray with their lunch bill. "Señor Platinum says lunch is on him."

"I can't stand this," Dana said.

"What?" Ashley asked, confused.

"Now, on top of everything, Peggy Braden has given you worldwide buying power? There is positive energy and then there is plain dumb luck."

Ashley rolled her eyes. "Here we go again. Maggie, you've known me since seventh grade. Tell her I'm not lucky."

"Well, you were voted prom queen at Franklin High," Maggie answered.

"So?"

"We went to Jefferson," Maggie said gently.

"That doesn't mean anything," Ashley insisted, as she added a big tip and signed the bill.

"Thank you, Ashley," said Zuki.

Ashley nodded.

"Face it, babe," Dana said. "When they whacked you with that lucky stick — they whacked you good."

"You guys are crazy." Ashley got up to leave.

Dana's face lit up. "Okay," she said, opening the door to the street. "If you don't think you have the luck gene, then you wouldn't mind taking a little test."

"Test?" asked Ashley.

They passed a newsstand. Dana held out a

dollar. "One scratch-off ticket, please," she said to the cashier.

The cashier pointed to dozens of different scratch-off lottery tickets. "Which one?"

Dana turned to Ashley. "Do you want to pick one?"

"No. This is not a fair test. I happen to be very good at these."

"It's the lottery. Nobody's supposed to be good at it."

Maggie pointed to a ticket. "The green one, please," she said.

Moments later, Dana and Maggie watched Ashley count her winnings.

"Five, ten, fifteen," she counted. "I told you."

"How do you do it, Ash?" Maggie asked.

Ashley shrugged. "You just scratch the silver boxes."

"Scratch!" Dana screamed. "You just scratch!"

Dana pretended to bite Ashley's shoulder. Maggie punched her playfully.

"Ow! Hey, easy! I can't afford to be injured. I've got a major event to plan." Ashley checked her watch. "And we have a walk-through with Peggy, downtown, in ten minutes."

"Taxi!" Dana yelled, holding out her hand. "We'll never make it."

"Negativity," Ashley said, getting into a cab. "*That's* your problem."

Maggie waved good-bye from the sidewalk. "Make Mommy proud, girls."

Ashley and Dana set up posters for their presentation in the Palace — one of New York City's most spectacular ballrooms.

Two huge doors opened. Peggy Braden and her entourage entered.

"This place is amazing!" Peggy said, taking in the glittery sophistication.

"Hi, Ms. Braden, um, Peggy. Are you ready to be impressed?" Ashley asked.

"I'm ready to have some questions," Peggy said.

"Of course. I would hope so," Ashley said, as she began to set the scene for the party. She swept her arms around the room. "We're going for a carnival-like atmosphere. An upscale mix of VIPs, celebs, and record industry insiders. Only everyone will wear masks." Ashley pulled a cool mask from behind her back and handed it to Peggy.

She walked toward a corner of the huge ballroom. "Over here is the VIP area." Ashley pointed across the dance floor. "There, a stage and screen with Masquerade's latest videos and professional dancers."

Ashley twirled around to face Peggy. "There will be fog and neon lights, circus performers, fortune-tellers, and sky dancers overhead!"

The expression on Peggy's face made it clear — she was impressed.

Ashley's voice rose. "It's going to be a magical night!"

*Chapter Eight

It *was* a magical night *and* an amazing party. Ashley, dressed to kill in a flitty, V-neck Balenciaga champagne silk charmeuse dress and strappy Jimmy Choo stilettos, was the center of it all. Her mask was exquisite — a champagne mesh veil with rhinestones and feathers that concealed her eyes. She greeted guests and VIPs, feeling only slightly guilty when Sarah Jessica Parker stopped to say hello. She kept the entertainment going and made sure Damon Phillips's champagne glass was constantly refilled. She beamed when she saw Peggy, sporting a gold-and-black feathered mask, happily accept a drink from a waiter walking on stilts.

A moment later, the Dragon Lady came up behind her. "The hired dancers," Peggy said.

"Are doing their thing," Ashley cheerfully responded.

"And Phillips?"

"Is happy and goes on in five minutes. Peggy, I'm on it," Ashley said.

"See that you are, my dear."

Ashley watched Peggy head back to the party and spoke into her headset. "Let's ease up on the fog. It's getting too thick."

"Sure thing, boss," Dana drawled into her own headset. She stood right next to Ashley.

Ashley turned to her with a big smile. "Aren't headsets fun?"

Antonio walked toward Ashley, putting his black, Zorro-like eye mask on. "Which one is she?" he asked.

Ashley pointed to Peggy.

"Her? Nice," he said.

"She's a little high-strung," Ashley said.

"No problem," Antonio said. "But that's going to cost you extra."

Ashley laughed and pushed him in Peggy's direction. "You're terrible. And a doll. Now go, I have work to do." A voice came over her headset, and Ashley turned aside. "What? No! If they're not on the guest list they're not getting in!"

Outside, guests arrived in masquerade costume. Paparazzi snapped photos. And Jake tried to sneak in.

"All right! All right!" Jake yelled as he was shoved past the welcome sign:

THE DOWNTOWN MASQUERADE BASH
SUPPORTING THE SECOND STREET SHELTER

"Hey, easy on the coat!"

Burly security guards tossed Jake to the curb. Two models in stiletto heels stepped over him, heading for the party. Jake recognized them from the pages of glossy magazines and Times Square billboards.

"What a nobody," said the first.

The second squinted at Jake as he tried to stand. "Ugh." She winced. "Total nobody."

Jake brushed himself off with as much dignity as he could and sprinted down an alley — away from the lights and the people and toward the stage door.

"Hold the door," he shouted to a caterer, who was carrying in the last few boxes of gourmet hors d'oeuvres. Jake had one foot in the door before another security guard stopped him, clipboard in hand.

"Are you Ronald?" he asked.

Jake saw his chance. "Yes. That's me. Ronald."

"You're late. Dancers change in room five. Then get your cute little groove thing out on the floor."

Jake almost ran into the door, trying to act like he might actually have a cute little groove thing.

✳ Chapter Nine

Ashley walked past Madame Z, the tarot card reader. The exotic gypsy read the cards for a masked couple. The woman waved to Ashley.

"Ashley!" Peggy took off her mask and beamed at her.

"Peggy. Antonio. I see you two are really hitting it off," Ashley said.

"We are. We really are," Antonio answered, kissing Peggy's hand. "Thanks for setting us up."

"*You* set us up?" Peggy asked.

"Guilty as charged," Ashley said with a nervous grin.

"Well, thank you. He's adorable," Peggy answered.

"My pleasure," Ashley said, relaxing. "You look made for each other."

Peggy beamed even brighter. "That's what Madame Z just said!"

"Did she?" Ashley answered.

"Come." Antonio took Peggy's arm and led her onto the dance floor. "We must dance."

Ashley's jaw dropped. "Wow." She turned to Madame Z. "Keep up the good work."

Madame Z flipped a card with her ringed finger and examined Ashley's face. "Sit, please," she said in a heavy accent.

Ashley hesitated. She had a party to monitor.

"Don't you want Madame Z to tell you what is in the cards?"

"No, thanks. Save it for the guests."

"Ah, a skeptic."

"No. It's just how many times can you hear 'You will meet a handsome stranger'? Hello! It's called a Tuesday," Ashley said.

"And you think your good fortune is normal?" Madame Z asked. She flipped over another card. "Ah, as I suspected."

"What did it say?" Ashley sat. "Am I going to win a cruise? Because lately I've had this cruise-winning feeling."

"Not exactly. Fortune and luck have spun your

way. But the wheel may be spinning back," Madame Z said mysteriously.

Ashley noticed that Peggy and Antonio had disappeared into the crowd of dancers. "I'm sorry, but I really don't have time for spinning wheels." She stopped to listen to her headset for a moment. "I have five hundred guests and a broken bubble cannon to attend to."

"Then go." Madame Z waved her jeweled hands. "But know this," she warned. "Those who don't appreciate their good fortune risk losing it to another."

"Uh-huh," Ashley answered, not really listening. "Keep up the good work, Z. The other guests are really eating this stuff up. Later." Ashley went in search of the bubble cannon.

Madame Z followed Ashley with her eyes. She flipped over another card and jumped to her feet. "Holy cow!"

Jake, wearing a tuxedo and a red cummerbund, stood with a group of identically dressed dancers. As they headed out to the dance floor, Jake slipped off to the side and found his backpack. He kissed his rabbit's foot for luck and grabbed a McFly CD.

Damon Phillips was just taking the stage. "Is everyone having a good time?" he asked.

The question was met with a huge round of applause from the guests. Jake worked his way through the crowd as Phillips made his speech.

"I want to thank everyone for coming out here to support the Second Street Shelter. So far, we have collected two hundred and seventy thousand dollars. But I want more! Get yourselves over to the auction and show me the money!"

Phillips's speech was met with another huge round of applause. Ashley cued the music and watched Peggy and Antonio sneak away together.

"Do you think I should slip him one of my songs?" Maggie asked, nodding toward Phillips.

"Why not? What have you got to lose?" Ashley said.

"Umm," Maggie said to herself, with a queasy expression. "My lunch. My dignity. My hopes. My dreams."

Ashley spoke into her headset. "I need my dancers to get more people onto the dance floor. But be fabulous and gallant about it."

Maggie and Dana watched one of the dancers ask a guest to dance.

"That's what I want to see," Ashley said, when the guest accepted.

Jake, clutching the McFly CD, ignored Ashley's orders. He was headed straight for Damon Phillips in the VIP area.

"Hold it." Dana stopped him.

Jake stopped short, hiding the CD behind his back. "Me?"

"All dancers are supposed to be on the dance floor. And the dance floor is that way." She pointed in the opposite direction.

"Ah. I . . . sure . . ." Jake, eyes on Phillips, didn't notice Ashley's headset. "I was just going to ask this lovely guest to dance."

The girls laughed.

"Oh," Ashley said. "Sucking up to the boss, huh?"

"Sorry?" Jake asked, still preoccupied with Phillips.

"Oh, go for it," Maggie said, giving Ashley a small shove. "Enjoy."

"You know what," Ashley said. "I will. I deserve to have a little fun tonight."

Jake tucked the CD into his cummerbund and tripped over a step leading to the dance floor.

Ashley turned and smiled at him — a stunning

smile, ready for fun. Jake smiled back, and Ashley noticed for the first time just how cute he was. Electricity charged between them, but the music was too loud for talking, even for exchanging names. Strobe lights flashed. Colored lights swept the room and fog rolled across the crowded dance floor. All of Ashley's carefully planned details came together to create a magical moment.

Madame Z watched Ashley and Jake twirl around the dance floor, then flipped over another tarot card — a picture of two crossed shooting stars.

✳ Chapter Ten

The dancers crowded Ashley and Jake, pushing them closer together. Jake took Ashley in his arms, and they danced like they were the only couple in the room — the only couple on Earth. The music swelled and Ashley leaned forward for a kiss at the same moment that confetti began to rain on them from above. It was a supernatural, tingling-in-her-toes, butterflies-in-her-stomach kind of a kiss.

Ashley leaned back, stunned. "Sorry, I —"

"No," Jake said. "I'm sorry."

Still reeling from what felt like the world's most perfect kiss, Jake saw Phillips leaving the VIP area and heading for the door. "I have to go."

"But —"

"There's something I have to take care of." Jake hesitated for a moment, but this was his last chance to get McFly's CD into Phillips's hands. "But I promise I'll be right back." He rushed for the door, jumping over the step he had tripped on earlier.

Maggie rushed to Ashley's side. "Who was *that?*"

"I honestly don't know," Ashley answered, still dazed by the kiss.

"Weren't you just *kissing* that guy you honestly don't know?"

"Yeah," Ashley murmured, losing him in the crowd.

She and Maggie left the dance floor. Ashley tripped over the step and broke her heel. She leaned down to fix it.

Riiiiiip.

Suddenly, there was a new side slit in Ashley's dress that hadn't been there before.

Jake raced out of the Palace and searched for Phillips. He spotted him having an intense conversation on his cell phone — so intense that Phillips didn't even notice that he had stepped into traffic.

A delivery truck sped toward him. The driver hit his brakes with loud screech. Less than a second before the truck would have hit him, Jake yanked Phillips back onto the sidewalk. The force threw

Jake forward right into the truck. He hit the ground — hard.

The driver jumped out of his truck. A crowd gathered.

Jake stood, checking his arms and legs, making sure nothing was broken. "I'm okay," he whispered to himself, stunned. "I'm okay," he said to the driver.

"Are you sure? Somebody call 911."

"No," Jake said, still not entirely believing it himself. "I'm okay. Really. I'm fine."

The driver stared at his truck, then at Jake. "Well then, you're the luckiest guy I've ever seen."

Jake almost laughed at the idea that someone — anyone — would think he was lucky. Then he noticed that Phillips was still in shock. "Are *you* okay?" he asked.

Phillips snapped out of his daze. "I'm more than okay. I'm alive. You saved my life, Spider-Man."

"It was nothing." Jake shrugged.

"No. It was something. I have to make this up to you. Anything. You name it."

"I'm just glad you're okay," Jake answered.

"C'mon. There has to be something I could do for you."

"Okay. I know this might be pushing my luck,

and I really don't want to put you out, but —" Jake pulled out the McFly CD.

Before he could say anything more, Phillips spoke. "Okay."

Expecting his usual rejection, Phillips's okay didn't register. "Please," Jake said. "This band is really — what did you say?"

Phillips took the CD. "I said okay. No problem. Bring" — he stopped to read the CD — "McFly by the office and we'll have a listen."

"Thank you, Mr. Phillips! Thank you so much!"

They shook hands. Phillips was on his way back into the party when he suddenly turned around. "Hey! What's your name?"

"Jake. Jake Hardin."

"I owe you big, Jake Hardin."

This can't be happening, Jake thought. "Is it me?" he asked himself. "Or did I just get lucky?"

✳ Chapter Eleven

"Help! Help! She's choking," Maggie screamed.

Ashley desperately gasped for breath, her eyes wide and her hands up in front of her throat. Maggie thumped her on the back, but it didn't help.

Dana, hearing Maggie's screams, pushed her way through the crowd. She put her arms around Ashley's waist from behind with her fist just below Ashley's rib cage. With a quick thrust she performed the Heimlich maneuver. An olive flew out of Ashley's mouth and hit Maggie in the face.

"What was that?" Dana asked.

"Olive," said Maggie.

Ashley still gasped for breath. "That was scary."

Dana stood back and eyed Ashley from head to toe. "And what happened to your dress?"

Ashley stressed. "Is it really noticeable?"

"You can hardly tell," Maggie said.

There was a commotion from across the room.

"What the —" Dana listened to her headset for a moment. "Ashley, you'd better look at this."

The three best friends turned to see two New York City police officers putting handcuffs on Peggy and Antonio. Peggy glared at Ashley. A police officer walked toward her.

"Ashley Albright?" he asked.

"I'm afraid to say yes," she answered.

"You're under arrest. You have the right to remain silent." The officer pulled Ashley's arms behind her, slapped a pair of handcuffs on her, and finished reading her rights.

Dana and Maggie stood staring — shocked and scared — with no idea how to help their friend.

"No. No. No," Ashley said. "I obey the law. I like the law. What did I —" Suddenly Ashley realized what it was, and it was an easy problem to fix. She tried to smile at the officer. "Is this about Sarah Jessica Parker's dry cleaning? 'Cause that was a mistake. I'm going to return it as soon as . . ."

The detective marched Ashley across the floor toward Peggy and Antonio. The three of them were rushed past a group of paparazzi, reporters, and Damon Phillips and into police cars.

"You're a criminal?" Ashley shouted at Antonio as her mug shot was taken.

Antonio stepped up for his turn in front of the camera. "I thought you knew," he said calmly. He smiled big for the camera.

Peggy was next. She stared straight at the lens, furious. "If I go down, Ashley, you go down. And even if I don't go down, you're still going down."

A few minutes later, in a holding cell surrounded by scary-looking women, Peggy focused on Ashley again. "I have never been so humiliated."

"But I didn't . . ." Ashley responded weakly. Then she broke into a big smile.

"What are you grinning about?" Peggy barked.

"I know what's going on here," Ashley teased.

"What?" Peggy snapped.

"Where is he?" Ashley asked.

"Who?"

"The host," Ashley said.

"The host of what?" Peggy was mad enough to reach out and strangle her protégé.

"This reality show!" Ashley said. She yelled

through the cell bars. "I figured it out! You can come out now and tell me what I won!"

"Are you insane?" Peggy asked.

"Peggy, you are a great boss, but a lousy actress. I watch enough TV to know which way the wind blows." She yelled through the bars again, "Guys, did David Pennington put you up to this?"

A tough girl walked up to Ashley and stood over her with a sneer. "That's my seat."

"I'm sorry," Ashley said, still waiting for someone to show up with a camera and yell, "Gotcha!" "I thought this was festival seating."

Peggy grabbed Ashley and shook her. "This is *real life*, Ashley. You not only cost me my biggest client, but I can't even imagine what they are going to say about me in the *New York Post*."

Ashley stared, still not understanding.

A guard came to the cell door. "Braden," he yelled. "You've made bail."

Peggy took a deep breath, raised her head, and threw back her shoulders. "Oh, and in case you haven't guessed. You're fired." She spun on her heel and left the cell, leaving Ashley alone.

Ashley leaned against the graffiti-covered wall. The tough girl scowled at her.

"That's my wall," she said, starting to rise.

Ashley stepped away from the wall. "Is this your floor?" she asked.

The other prisoners let out an "Ooooooh!" The girl moved toward Ashley. The next thing she knew, there was a fist in her face. As everything went black, Ashley thought she heard B. B. King's "Bad Luck" playing in the background.

✳ Chapter Twelve

The next morning, Ashley left the police station in a battered trench coat one of the officers had found in the pile of clothes that were usually passed out to homeless people. A bandage covered her nose, but at least it had stopped bleeding.

Thunder boomed overhead and the sky opened, drenching Ashley in cold rain. She waved at a passing cab. Instead of stopping, it sped by, hitting a huge puddle. In seconds the luckiest girl in the world was drenched — and spitting muddy water out of her mouth.

After a long, wet walk home, Ashley gave a weary hello to Oscar. He didn't recognize her for a moment, then held open the door. She waited at least ten minutes for the elevator, and finally trudged down the hall to her apartment.

Two uniformed cops stood just inside the front door. A half-dozen workers wearing "Hazardous Materials" bio suits and masks had just finished bagging the entire contents of Ashley's apartment.

Ashley watched openmouthed as firemen hacked at the walls and ceilings with axes. "Oh, my goodness."

"Is this your apartment?" asked one of the Hazmat guys.

Ashley nodded. "What happened?"

The man shrugged. "Flood."

"Flood?" Ashley asked.

"It's a technical term for a lot of water where it shouldn't be. It's no big deal, though. We'll take care of it."

"Great. Thank you," Ashley said, relieved. "Can I go in and change my clothes?"

The man cracked up. He turned to his coworkers. "She wants to go in and change her clothes. Funny, huh? Jay Leno could do that joke."

"Why are you laughing?" Ashley asked. Nervousness gnawed at her stomach. If this wasn't a reality show, what was happening?

"Sweetheart, you've got a grade-four mold infestation. Life-threatening. Unfit for human habitation. You're lucky we found it."

"Lucky, yeah right," Ashley said. "But what about my stuff? My clothes. My furniture?"

"Don't worry about that," the Hazmat man answered.

"Thank goodness!" Ashley leaned against the wall with a sigh of relief.

"We'll burn it before it can contaminate anyone else."

Ashley stood tall, remembering Peggy's dignity as she swept out the jail cell. She tried to be upbeat. And dignified. "Oh. Good."

"We did manage to save these." The man handed Ashley a small, cardboard box.

"Thank you," Ashley said.

She walked toward the elevator. Just as the doors closed on the ghastly scene in her apartment, the bottom fell out of the box. The contents shattered on the elevator floor.

✳ Chapter Thirteen

McFly jammed in Downtown Masquerade Record's top-of-the-line recording studio. Photos of incredibly talented and famous artists, from jazz to rap and hip-hop, lined the walls.

Tom and the boys played and sang their best song:

> *"Everyone asks me.*
> *Who is she?*
> *Weird-o with five colors*
> *in her hair."*

Jake watched from the glassed-in control room. Damon Phillips keyed his BlackBerry and two of his followers listened, stone-faced. Jake wondered if Damon was even listening.

Tiffany, Phillips's assistant, handed out cups of coffee.

Suddenly, Phillips stood. "All right," he said. "Enough."

McFly was only fifteen seconds into their song. Jake signaled them to stop playing. He sat, stunned, as Phillips left the room with his followers.

"Go with him," Tiffany urged.

Phillips charged through the office. Jake ran behind. He caught up just as Phillips pushed through double glass doors.

"I'm sorry if that wasn't exactly —"

Phillips cut him off. "What do you like about them?"

"They're a fresh take on a retro sound. Like early Beatles meets Blink 182."

"I'm surprised you don't talk about record sales and demographics." Phillips barreled outside with his entourage.

Jake ran to keep up. "I think a band that's good will sell itself."

"A purist and an idealist," Phillips said. "I like that. I was once like that. Then I decided to become filthy rich." He stopped in front of his limo.

"Thanks for the opportunity," Jake said, shoulders slumping. This wasn't going to happen.

"Look," Phillips said. "I believe in luck. So I'm going to send the song to the radio, see how it plays. Meanwhile, you spend the next couple of weeks working on your follow-up."

"You mean you're signing the band?" Jake's forehead crinkled. He had no idea what was happening.

"I just spent eight minutes with you," Phillips answered with a wave of the hand. "Why would I waste that time if I wasn't signing the band?"

He turned to Tiffany, one foot in the limo. "Tiffany, have accounting cut an advance check and put them up in the artist's penthouse." Phillips pulled the limo door closed, and the car pulled away.

Tiffany turned to Jake with a big smile. "Congratulations."

Ashley, wearing Maggie's funky clothes instead of one of her own chic outfits, took a last bite of her sushi.

"I'm sorry, Ashley," Zuki said. "Your Visa has been declined, too."

"What's that," Ashley said miserably, "like the word of the day?"

Zuki tried to cheer her up. "What about Señor Platinum?"

"No. He got revoked when I got fired." She rooted through her wallet. "Here, try this one."

"Wow!" Zuki said. "Crunch Gym trial membership! You, me. Let's take this and hit Barneys! We can buy new fur coats and fancy skin cream like Julia Roberts uses!"

"Zuki . . ."

But Zuki was clearly enjoying himself. "Then, if there's any money left, we'll get some unnecessary cosmetic surgery. How do you think I'll look with a chin dimple?"

"Are you through?" Ashley asked.

"Lighten up, Ashley! Only joking! You have been a loyal customer for a long time."

Ashley brightened a bit. Maybe her luck was coming back. Zuki would give her a free lunch.

But suddenly Zuki was dead serious. "We'll give you six hours to pay."

✳ Chapter Fourteen

Ashley read the banner on the wall behind the bank teller:

WE'RE THE FRIENDLY BANK
WE CAN'T SAY NO!

"No," the bank teller said.

"I couldn't have spent *all* of it," Ashley said.

The teller checked her computer. "Actually, it looks like you spent more than all of it. Could I see your credit cards, please?"

"Yes. Thank you. These need fixing."

The teller took Ashley's cards and cut them all in half, throwing the pieces into the trash.

Jake and Katy stepped up to another teller's window. Jake handed her a check. Katy had a Band-Aid on her forehead and a splint on her finger.

"I just opened this account," Jake said. "And I'd like to get some cash." He steeled himself for rejection.

"How much?" the teller asked, all smiles.

Jake turned to Katy.

"Two hundred?" she said.

The teller nodded. "How would you like that?"

Jake and Katy high-fived, like they had just scored a touchdown at a championship football game.

"Twenties," Jake said. "And could I have a receipt? I think I want to frame it."

"Sure thing." The teller laughed. "Would you like a mint?"

"The bank is offering me a free mint! I have made it!"

"Careful." Katy pointed at her throat. "Choking hazard."

"Excellent point. You are truly wise beyond your years. Speaking of which . . ." Jake pulled out a charm bracelet and fastened it to Katy's wrist, carefully avoiding her finger splint. "Belated birthday present. May you be as lucky as I seem to be lately."

Stylish, successful, and totally fabulous — Ashley Albright's got all the luck.

Meeting cute guys is just par for the course.

Who else but Ashley would accidentally end up with Sarah Jessica Parker's dry cleaning?

While Ashley takes her good fortune for granted, Jake Harden appreciates what little luck he can find. Unfortunately it's usually spoiled—or soiled— by something.

But when she meets a mysterious stranger at the masquerade ball, Ashley has no idea that her luck's about to change. Who knew that one little kiss could pack such a punch?

Ashley wants her luck back, and she wants it back now. Madame Z is her only hope.

Dana and Maggie help Ashley search for the man with the luck-swapping smooch.

Ashley resorts to scratch-and-win lotto tickets to test out her luck, but all she gets is silver stuff under her nails.

Running low on funds helps Ashley develop an appreciation for the simpler things in life. Nothing beats pizza, a cozy apartment, and good friends.

After landing a
job at the Rock 'N' Bowl, it
seems Ashley's luck might
be coming back . . .

. . . but, then again, maybe not.

Jake helps Ashley deal with being completely jinxed—something he has plenty of experience with.

Hello, corporate credit card! Maybe things for Ashley are turning around after all!

Having a sweet boy like Jake around makes Ashley feel like the luckiest girl in the world.

"Your dad is so sweet," said the teller.

"Oh, no. She's not . . ." Jake said.

"Jake's my *pal*," said Katy.

"Well, it was great to meet you both. And, Jake, if you have any other banking needs . . ." The teller slipped him a piece of paper. It had her home telephone number on it. "I'm up late."

"Okay," said Jake. Girls didn't usually give him their phone numbers. He didn't quite know what to do.

The teller pointed to her name tag. "Judy," she said.

Jake pocketed the phone number with a grin.

Katy grabbed his arm. "C'mon, stud," she teased. "Let's go spend those twenty-dollar bills!"

On the other side of the bank, Ashley sat across from a loan officer.

"Just a little loan," she said, pretending to be cheerful.

"A little loan?"

Ashley nodded. "Just a pinch of money. That should hold me over."

The loan officer sighed and tried to explain how loans worked. "Generally, if someone wants a loan, they provide a specific reason. Like, I want a house. Or I'm paying for college."

"Oh, a house would be awesome," Ashley said.

"So it's for a house?"

"Look, I just need a little cash to carry me over between windfalls."

"Windfalls?" Now the loan officer was really confused.

"Yeah, you know," Ashley said. "Large sums of unexpected money?"

"Of course." The loan officer straightened the papers on his desk and wondered why he got stuck with all the crazies.

Ashley turned on the charm big-time, pushing her hair back and flashing him one of her biggest, brightest smiles. "C'mon. I'm good for it. How about this — I could even pay back a little more money than you loan me." She leaned back in her chair, satisfied that she had made a good case.

"You mean like *interest*?"

Ashley put her finger on her nose and winked.

"I'm sorry."

"Don't be sorry," Ashley said. "Work with me here." She stopped to read his name tag. "Richard."

Richard stood. "I have other customers."

Asking hadn't worked. Charm hadn't worked. Ashley had one more thing to try. She cried.

"Look." She sniffled. "I owe people money. These sushi guys have knives. . . ."

Richard crossed his arms. He wasn't going to budge.

Ashley panicked. She jumped to her feet and took off her shoes. "I can give you these as collateral. Manolo Blahniks. I mean, they're last season, but still."

Richard continued to stare, unmoving.

"I'm done playing games." Ashley held her shoe like a weapon, pointing the stiletto heel in Richard's face. "Either you put cash in my hands in ten seconds or else I'm going to . . ."

Richard pointed. Big security guards stood on either side of Ashley.

"What does it feel like when you're about to faint?" Ashley asked.

"Light-headed. Nausea," Richard said.

"Numbness in your legs," added one of the guards.

"Got it." Ashley fell to the ground. Her world went dark.

✳ Chapter Fifteen

Tiffany stood over Jake. "Are you okay?" she asked.

Jake lay on the floor, staring up at the ceiling. "This? This is my new apartment?"

The penthouse was a rock group's dream. Platinum records lined one wall. Guitars of famous musicians lined another.

"I know, it's pretty amazing. And at night, with the lights down low and the fireplace going . . . well, let's just say this place is totally romantic."

Was Tiffany flirting? Jake wondered. With him? "It's pretty — you know — in broad daylight."

Tiffany bounced on the couch. "And just so you know, Downtown Masquerade Records is a real nice place to work. Like, at some companies they don't let the employees date each other." She gazed into Jake's eyes. "Here, they do."

Jake gulped. That was pretty definitely flirting.

"So I'd better get back to work. See you around . . . Spider-Man." She gave Jake one last look and was off.

Downtown, on funky St. Mark's Place, Ashley thanked her best friends.

"It's so nice of you guys to let me stay here," she said. She didn't mention that it was the smallest apartment she had ever seen — hardly even big enough for Maggie's black cat, Pancakes. Maggie's guitar and keyboard sat in the corner, and took up half the room. Stuff was piled everywhere — Dana's books, Maggie's clothes. Ashley wondered how they ever found anything.

But just out of the bath, wrapped in a warm robe, Ashley felt better. Dana and Maggie were in their pajamas, listening to the story of Ashley's horrible day, nodding and expressing sympathy in all the right places.

All the while she complained, Ashley put on makeup and chose clothes from their closet. It was almost like a sleepover.

"Not only am I broke, but the Dragon Lady blacklisted me from every firm in the city."

"Why don't you phone your parents?" Dana suggested.

"And admit defeat? No way."

Maggie grabbed Ashley's hand and pulled it toward her. "What's that silver stuff under your fingernails?"

"Nothing." Ashley moved her hand behind her back.

"You've been doing those lottery scratchers, haven't you?" Dana said.

"No biggie," Ashley said. "I can quit anytime I want." She changed the subject, looking around the small apartment. "Where am I going to sleep?"

Maggie and Dana eyed each other and tried to sound upbeat.

"In your room," Maggie said.

"My room?" Had Maggie gone insane? Ashley wondered. This tiny room was all there was.

"Well," Maggie said. "My room is up there over the kitchen." She pointed to a small, home-made loft.

"And my room is the Jennifer Convertible under the window," Dana added.

"You can pick either the futon or the La-Z-Boy for your room," Maggie said cheerfully.

Ashley sighed. "My room is a futon. Perfect. They are really good for your back, right?"

"Might be," Maggie said. "All I know for sure is that they are free when you find them in an alley."

Ashley tried to look upbeat. "Great. I won't get in the way. You guys won't even know I'm here. Blow-dryer?"

"Next to the sink." Dana pointed.

Ashley went into the tiny bathroom, passing Maggie's cat. "I never noticed," she said, "is Pancakes *all* black?"

"Yeah. Why?"

"Just curious," Ashley answered. She checked herself out in the mirror and plugged in the hair dryer. "This is nice. We'll have fun. Everything is going to be o —"

Ashley turned on the blow-dryer and looked in the mirror again. "Oh, no!" she screamed. She moved in closer. "A zit! I have a zit!" Suddenly Ashley's hair was sucked into the back of the dryer. She yanked the dryer away and it hit the mirror.

Crack.

The mirror broke.

"Uh-oh," Ashley said.

The blow-dryer sparked and caught fire. Ashley threw it into the bathtub and turned on the water. In seconds a fuse blew and the whole apartment went dark. Turning, Ashley saw all the lights on St. Mark's Place go out, one by one. She had caused a blackout.

"My bad."

Maggie and Dana stumbled around, looking for candles. Maggie found Ashley sitting on the bathroom floor.

"Ash? Are you all right?"

"What is happening to me?" Ashley cried. "Everything I touch is ruined. Ever since the Masquerade Bash, I'm like the anti-Midas."

Dana hugged her.

"Ashley, my friend, for some reason the fates have dealt you a lousy hand. But the wheel always spins back, right?"

Dana's statement hit her like a ton of bricks. *Madame Z!* Ashley jumped to her feet, almost stepping on Pancakes in the dark bathroom. "That's it! I need to borrow some clothes."

*Chapter Sixteen

Madame Z carried her trash to the curb. The purple neon FORTUNE-TELLER sign was still lit in her window, but it was almost time to close up shop for the night.

Ashley stormed past and started banging on the door. "Madame Z," she called.

"Hello? Yes?"

Ashley whirled around. "You! You ruined my life!"

"What?"

"Everything in my life was perfect, and then you came around and —"

Madame Z interrupted her with a question. "Was it really perfect?"

Ashley was furious. "Oh, no. Don't you

psychoanalyze me. Just do your voodoo magic and give me my life back."

The fortune-teller waved her ringed fingers and made a spooky noise.

"All right. It's back. Now go. Madame Z is very tired."

"Don't patronize me." Ashley stamped her foot. "You and your cards screwed everything up and you have got to fix it."

"I tried to warn you. Did anything *unusual* happen at the party?"

"Besides my dress getting ripped, nearly choking to death, and felony charges for harboring a criminal?" Ashley snapped. "No."

"Nothing?" Madame Z asked. "How about before that?"

"I kissed a cute boy," she said. "But that's hardly unusual." Ashley looked away while she ran over the events of the evening in her mind. "Wait! You said right before that I could lose my luck to someone else? Is that what happened? Could he have —" She shook her head, hardly believing what she was asking. "Could he have somehow taken my luck?"

"Perhaps he needed it more than you." Madame Z moved around Ashley, toward her door.

"So he stole it!" Ashley's face flushed with anger. "That whack little kissing bandit. Well, he's *not* keeping my luck. You tell me right now how to get it back."

"If he took it from you with a kiss, then it stands to reason . . ." Madame Z smiled and closed the door.

The purple FORTUNE-TELLER light flickered across Ashley's face as she realized what she had to do, then it went dark.

Maggie struggled to push her mail cart down the hall. "This is insane!" she whispered.

"No it's not. I need a list of the dancers from the party, and if you could have found it on your own," Ashley whispered from the bottom of the cart, "I wouldn't have to be here." She held a package over her head.

"If Ms. Braden sees you, she'll go berserk!"

"Don't you want the old me back?" Ashley asked.

Maggie stopped to think about a life with an unlucky Ashley.

"Look, it's simple," Ashley said. "I just have to find the guy I kissed at the party and lay another wet one on him. Then the supernatural unicorn, hobbit, karma juices, or whatever will pass between us, and I will be the old me again."

"Sounds scientific," Maggie said.

"Madame Z said . . ."

"Yeah, I got that part. What I want to know is why you believe her." Maggie gave the cart another push.

"Because she's spooky," Ashley answered. "And it's the only explanation."

"Wait. Shhhh."

Peggy Braden walked down the hall, right toward Maggie.

"Hi, Ms. Braden." Maggie was way too cheerful.

Ashley tried to scrunch her body down even more.

"Who are you?" Peggy asked.

"Maggie. I'm in the mail room?" she answered, her voice rising.

A mail room worker wasn't important enough to pay attention to. "Right. Right." Peggy dismissed her. She continued down the hall, then stopped short. "Did DHL arrive yet?"

Maggie froze. "Uhh. Yes."

Maggie searched the cart, but the package Peggy was looking for was the same one Ashley was holding over her head. Maggie tugged on the package. Ashley tugged back. Peggy was getting closer. Finally Maggie yanked the package out of the cart, at the same time dumping a huge pile of mail on top of Ashley.

She whirled around, blocking the cart, and handed the package over with a big smile. "Here you go, Peggy."

Peggy's eyes narrowed.

"Ms. Braden," Maggie said more quietly.

As Peggy turned to leave, Maggie kicked the cart.

"Ouch!" Ashley said.

"Thanks to you, now Dragon Lady knows my name. I don't want her knowing my name, because then she can fire me," Maggie whispered. "Let's get your stupid dancer list, and I'll kill you later."

"One of these guy's lips are the key to getting my life back." Ashley dodged a bicycle messenger, then an open pothole.

Dana looked at the head shots in Ashley's hands. "I don't believe it," she said.

"See. It's ridiculous!" Maggie said. "Kisses don't change luck."

"No," Dana answered. "I don't believe how cute these guys are!" She nudged Ashley's shoulder. "You go, girl!"

"Great," Maggie said, as she and Dana watched

Ashley almost get splashed by a passing truck. "Now you're encouraging her."

"Oh, I still think you're crazy," Dana said to Ashley. "I'm just here to observe and mock."

"Guys, please," Ashley said, jumping over a giant mound of dog poop, "I just want things back to the way they were."

"Then maybe you should consider looking for another job," Dana pointed out.

"One doesn't *look for* jobs. Jobs are *offered*. And I'll have plenty of options once the old me is back." Ashley stopped short, staring down at the sidewalk. "Holy — Did you see that? I could have stepped on that crack and broken my mother's back!"

"And given your dad a cataract," Dana said.

Ashley gasped, totally missing the joke. "That can happen, too? I need to put an end to this. Fast."

"How are you even going to know if you've kissed the right guy? You don't even know what he looks like," Dana said.

"I've got a foolproof test," Ashley announced, patting her purse.

Dana and Maggie eyed each other, convinced Ashley had lost her mind along with her luck. But just then, Ashley jumped.

"Ooh! Ooh!" she pointed. She checked his

picture against one of her head shots. "That's definitely him."

Dana and Maggie checked him out.

"When his office told you he was leaving on vacation tomorrow," Maggie said, "I didn't realize they meant his honeymoon."

The three girls stared at the bride and groom on the church steps, surrounded by cheering family and friends.

Ashley took a deep breath and headed toward them, dodging a speeding taxi. Dana and Maggie followed.

✳ Chapter Seventeen

Ashley, Dana, and Maggie joined the wedding guests in the front of the church. The bride and groom made their way down the line, accepting kisses and congratulations from friends and family.

The last relative took the groom's hand and kissed him on the cheek.

Ashley was next.

"Michael!" she said with a big smile. "Congratulations!" She pulled him toward her. Instead of pecking him on the cheek, like the wedding guests, Ashley kissed him on the lips. The groom's eyes got wide as he tried to pull away.

The bride's eyes got even wider.

Ashley broke away and pulled out a roll of lottery

scratchers. The groom stammered something to his bride.

"Gold bar, gold bar," Ashley said, scratching furiously. This was it! Her luck was — "Tomato. Shoot!" She tossed the card aside.

Ashley ran off in search of another dancer, followed by Dana and Maggie.

The bride and groom started their first argument.

A street performer, dressed in silver, stood completely still in the middle of Times Square. Each time someone put a dollar in his cup, he struck a new pose. Ashley ran up and kissed him. With silver lips she scratched a card. "Liberty Bell . . . joker . . . rats!" She crumpled the card and put it in the trash.

Ashley, photos in hand, slipped in the stage door of a Broadway theater. A line of dancers practiced a musical number. Ashley ran up, kissed one, and ran offstage again. She scratched a card — no luck. She turned to Dana for sympathy, but now Dana was kissing the dancer.

Ashley grabbed Dana's arm and pulled her offstage.

Ashley, carrying a bouquet of flowers, tiptoed into a hospital room. She pulled a thermometer out of a guy's mouth and puckered up.

Dana and Maggie cringed behind their surgical masks as Ashley laid a kiss on him.

She scratched a lottery ticket. "Sorry," it read. She ripped off another card for a second opinion, then a third, then a fourth.

Ashley jogged through Central Park, looking for her man. She spotted him across the Boat Pond. He bounced up and down so much that Ashley had trouble matching his stride. She waited for the perfect moment, then struck like a cobra.

"Ah!" she screamed as the confused jogger ran off. "He bi my ongue!"

Maggie and Dana were definitely NOT sympathetic.

Ashley scratched a ticket, trying to ignore her sore tongue. She showed it to Dana and Maggie.

"Loser," Maggie read.

Ashley held up the last head shot. It showed a guy named Tom Guthrie in four poses — dressed as a waiter, a tennis player, a nerd, and just as a handsome guy. "We have one left," she said.

"Tom Guthrie?" Maggie asked. "We've already looked for him at three different addresses."

"You're right." Ashley stared at the ground. "I should just give up. Face reality. I'm like the rest of the rabbit after they chop off its lucky foot."

"C'mon, Ash." Maggie put her arm around her best and oldest friend. "Things aren't that bad."

"You still have your friends," Dana added.

"Thanks," Ashley said. She moved to put her other arm around Dana, but Dana pulled away.

"It's probably best that we don't touch for a while," she said, blowing Ashley a kiss. "But I love you."

Back at the apartment, Dana clicked on the answering machine. Over the speaker, they heard a deep, male voice.

"Hey, Ash. It's David Pennington. It's been hard to find you. Anyway, you free tonight? Big opening at Gallery Muse. I'll see you there at seven. Bye."

"David Pennington? Another date?" Dana asked.

"I'm not going." Ashley flopped on the futon.

"It's another chance with a great guy!" Maggie said.

"It's a chance to get hit by a bus. Besides, your

black cat just crossed my path." She turned to Dana. "How does my horoscope look?"

Dana checked the newspaper. "Your moon is in Uranus."

"What does that mean?" The cat crossed Ashley's path again. Ashley moved away. "I'm sorry, Pancakes, but I can't be around you right now."

Maggie had had it with Ashley's doom and gloom. "Look, he could have canceled. But he didn't. Isn't that proof this bad-luck stuff is bogus?"

Ashley didn't even look up.

Maggie pulled her to her feet and gave her a good shake. "Ashley, unlucky girls don't get asked out by one of *US* magazine's ten most eligible bachelors. Unlucky girls watch as their more attractive friends get asked out while they stay at home watching *Oprah* and eating last year's Halloween candy."

"You're right," Ashley admitted.

"Of course I am."

"I'm not cursed. I'm just looking at things the wrong way." Ashley's face brightened. "These setbacks could be opportunities."

"Absolutely," Maggie said. "When one door closes . . ."

". . . two others open," Ashley chimed in.

Dana raised her eyebrows, not so sure. "Been known to happen," she said halfheartedly.

"Yup," Ashley said, getting pumped. "I'm turning over a new leaf. The good luck starts now!" She gasped. "My contact!"

Ashley pawed through the kitty litter, looking for the lens that had just bounced out of her eye. She blew it off and put it right back in.

Ashley wouldn't let a little thing like that get her down. "And the good luck officially starts . . . NOW!" she announced again.

Maggie looked at her, her face crumpled in concern. "Did you just put that back in your eye?"

✳ Chapter Eighteen

Ashley stood outside Gallery Muse. The gallery was full of modern sculptures, all made out of a similar earthy material. From the sidewalk it looked like grass, dirt, and clay, but Ashley couldn't tell for sure, and the woman at the door was being difficult — extremely difficult.

"I'm sorry, miss. But if you're not on the list, I can't let you in."

Ashley, wearing Maggie's clothes, tried to peer over the top of the woman's clipboard with her good eye.

"But I am on the list," she said. "I'm a 'plus one.' David Pennington, plus one."

The woman took in Ashley's eye patch — a leftover from Maggie's Halloween costume. "Not Blackbeard the pirate?"

Ashley saw David waving from inside.

"See. David Pennington. There!" She pointed.

David waved her in. The woman let Ashley pass, only Ashley walked right into the glass door. "Ouch," she said, bouncing off the glass.

Ashley moved cautiously, grabbing handrails and trying to stay on the lookout for anything that could go wrong.

"What happened to you?" David asked, helping her through the gallery.

Ashley tried to come up with a light and breezy reply, but she sounded more nervous than cool. "Me? Just a run of . . . bad luck, I guess. Jobs get lost, tongues get bitten, and did you know that stocks can actually *go down,* too?"

"I meant your eye." David grabbed Ashley's arm as she tripped over nothing.

"My eye? I'm sorry. I must look like a wreck. I should go. . . ."

"No. You look great. Like a cool pirate. Come on. I have a surprise for you."

Ashley smiled at David and tried to relax. Maybe things were turning around. "I love surprises."

David led her to a giant sculpture — like a huge, oozing, mud volcano — sitting in the middle of the floor.

Ashley cracked up. "Get a load of that!" She could hardly get the words out between giggles. "Ugly. Brown. Pile."

"Ashley?"

"It looks like it fell out of the rear end of an elephant." She laughed. "Is that mud?"

An elegant woman stepped out from behind the mud volcano.

"Ashley," David said. "Meet my mother . . . *the artist.*"

Ashley choked on her laugh. "Mrs. Pennington," she babbled. "I'm so . . . I had no idea I was going to meet you. What a" — she struggled to find a word — "surprise?" She turned to David. Was this it?

David nodded.

"You look so much younger in person," Ashley said, still babbling. "Not that you're old. And your work. It's very"— Ashley struggled again — "experimental."

Mrs. Pennington turned to her son. "If I'm going to have to listen to this, I'm going to need a drink," she said.

"Good idea. Waiter!" David called.

A man with a tray full of exotic drinks crossed

the room. He looked familiar. Ashley checked him out while Mrs. Pennington chose a drink.

"David, darling," Mrs. Pennington said. "It appears that awful critic from the *Times* is here."

Ashley opened her purse and looked at Tom Guthrie's crumpled head shot. The waiter was him! "No way," she said to herself. "This can't be happening."

Tom crossed the room, getting lost in the crowd.

"That waiter . . . he's —" Ashley said.

"More your type," Mrs. Pennington said. "I totally agree. A man in the service industry is quite a catch for a girl like you."

"Mother," David warned.

Ashley ignored the insult. She kept her eyes on Tom. "If you two don't mind, I'm going to run to the ladies' room."

Strange, freaky music started to play. Ashley cut through the crowd, searching for Tom. She cornered him as he started to climb onto a small pedestal. "You!" she said. "Finally!"

"Excuse me?"

Ashley took out her lipstick and reapplied it as if her life depended on it. "So, Tom Guthrie, how was your week?" she asked. "Anything *lucky* happen?"

Tom shrugged, confused. "The Knicks won," he said.

"You're welcome," Ashley answered. "Now remember, this is just business."

Ashley stepped in to kiss Tom as all the lights in the gallery went out.

The party chatter stopped. The room was completely quiet.

In the dark, Tom tripped backward on the step leading to the pedestal. Ashley fell on top of him.

A spotlight illuminated a waiter on a pedestal on the other side of the room.

"I am mud man," the waiter announced, tearing off his clothes. He was covered in brown body paint.

"Uh-oh," Ashley muttered.

Two spotlights hit two more waiters. They tore off their clothes.

Ashley tried to kiss Tom before the spotlight him them. Tom struggled to get away.

"I am mud man! We are mud men!" the waiters announced. "And he is our mud king!"

The spotlight hit Ashley and Tom as she struggled on top of him. All the eyes in the gallery, including David's and Mrs. Pennington's, stared at her.

Ashley thumped Tom on the chest. "Heart attack!" she lied. "I know CPR!"

"I'm not . . ." Tom said.

Ashley thumped him again. "He's not breathing!" she yelled.

Ashley slapped one hand over his mouth and clamped his nose closed with the other. She leaned in and administered a mouth-to-mouth kiss.

Tom gasped for breath.

"He's totally breathing," David said.

Ashley came up with another lie — quick. "That's a cardiac, um, reflex thing," she said to David. Then kissed Tom again. Tom stopped struggling. A moment later, they broke apart.

Tom was breathless. "Thank you," he said.

Ashley waved her arms dramatically. "He's going to be okay."

An awkward applause broke out in the gallery as Ashley climbed off the pedestal. Sure that she had her luck back, Ashley rejoined David and his mother.

"Lucky you were here," David said sarcastically.

"Lucky you know CPR," his mother added in the same tone of voice.

"That's me!" Ashley said with a confident smile. "Lucky. In fact, I'm feeling very . . ." She leaned against a mud sculpture. It started to tip. Then it toppled. Into the sculpture next to it.

Crash.

Boom.

Crunch.

Splat.

Like dominoes, the sculptures fell, one by one. The final figure toppled next to David, who jumped out of its way, knocking Ashley face-first into Mrs. Pennington's pile of mud.

The gallery was completely quiet, until Tom Guthrie called out, "Where is my mud queen?"

Flash!

Ashley, covered in mud, had her mug shot taken — again!

"It was an accident," she said.

Moments later, the bars clanged shut on the holding cell. Ashley turned to face her cell mates. The same tough girl as last week stood in front of her.

"This will absorb the blood," she said, throwing a blanket on the cement floor.

*Chapter Nineteen

The next morning, Ashley left the police station. She wandered the streets, sad, alone, and crusted in dried mud. She passed a diner. The food looked so good that even though she had no money, she went in.

Ashley flopped into a warm, dry booth. A waiter started toward her, but the manager stopped him and approached Ashley himself.

"What can I get you?" he asked.

Ashley looked at the menu, stalling for time. "Could I just have a glass of water?" she asked.

"Sparkling or flat?"

"Tap water?" Ashley asked.

"No buy. No sit." The owner quoted a sign that hung in the window. "See?"

"Yes," Ashley said, slumping farther into the booth. "I see."

Jake, at the table next to Ashley's, lowered his newspaper. He remembered what it was like to be cold, tired, and hungry.

"May I use the bathroom?" Ashley asked quietly.

"No buy. No bathroom," the owner answered. He pointed to another sign that said just that.

"Great. Fine," Ashley said, her voice rising. "I'm leaving. I'm leaving." She got up to go and noticed other customers staring at her.

"Are you enjoying the show?" she asked. "Oh, you think you see me, but you don't. No, the real me doesn't have days like this."

The whole room gawked at her.

"As a matter of fact," she continued, "maybe I'm not even here right now. This is probably all a dream I'm having, induced by a . . . by a massage!" She got caught up in her fantasy. "Yes! A massage that I won in a charity raffle. And it came with a full day of pampering, including a manicure, a pedicure, and a spa lunch!"

She eyed the leftovers on a customer's plate. "Man, that looks good. Are you done?"

The customer nervously offered Ashley his

leftovers, worried about what she would do if he said no.

"That was a joke! I'm not going to eat your scraps."

Ashley looked at the leftovers again. Her stomach growled. "Maybe just that." She grabbed a handful of French fries, then stopped, food hanging from her mouth. "Look at me! I've turned into a coyote! I'm leaving." She grabbed one more French fry and knocked over the salt.

"Perfect," she said, shaking her head. "Just so everyone knows," she announced to the still-staring customers, "I think what I am about to do is ridiculous, but it can't hurt, can it?"

Jake watched Ashley toss the salt over her shoulder, right into the owner's face.

"Agh!" he screamed. The man stumbled backward into a table, sending himself and the table crashing into the floor.

"That was an accident!" Ashley said.

Jake paid his check, quickly wrapped half of his sandwich in a napkin, and hurried Ashley out — all before the owner could get up. He took Ashley's arm and rushed her across the street.

"I couldn't help but overhear your —"

"Meltdown?" Ashley interrupted. "Broke, job-less, and I just ate *les frites d'un étranger.*"

"Excuse me?"

"A stranger's French fries. I thought it might sound better in French."

"Ah." Jake handed her his sandwich. "I thought maybe you could use this."

"Thank you." Ashley wanted to ram the whole thing into her mouth at once. She sat on a park bench and tried to eat slowly.

"Look, I know of a job. If that would help," Jake said.

"What's the scam?" Ashley asked, chewing.

"No scam."

"Do you want me to join your religion or some-thing?"

Jake laughed. "No. No religion stuff. Just a job. A bad job. Crummy pay for crummy hours."

"Sounds great," Ashley said. "But that doesn't answer my question. What's the scam?"

"Let's just say I know what it's like to be TOL."

"TOL?"

"Totally outta luck," Jake answered.

Ashley glared at him. "What makes you think I'm TOL? Just because I spilled the salt back there?"

Jake pointed to a small sign on the bench next to where Ashley sat: WET PAINT.

"Oh . . ."

"Look." Jake tried to be comforting. "Where you are right now . . . I've been there. More than been there. I was the *mayor* of there." He held out his hand to help Ashley up. "I'm Jake," he said.

Ashley stood and shook his hand. "I'm Ashley." She twisted around to see the green stripes across her already muddy back. "I don't think I'm dressed for a job interview," she said.

"For this one, you'll be fine," Jake answered. "You know," he said, leading her down the street, "I have a shirt and two pairs of pants that match that perfectly."

✳ Chapter Twenty

Ashley stood at the other end of the counter while Jake talked to Mac about a job. Jake's expression was grim.

"I didn't get it, did I?" Ashley asked when he joined her.

"No. It's not that," Jake answered. "You can have the job. But it's my old job."

"So?"

"So, I had hoped that Mac would hire you as a waitress or something. My old gig was sort of a janitor slash food-delivery person slash toilet attendant."

Ashley's look of disgust in response to the word "toilet" said it all. "Do I really look that desperate?"

"Well . . ." Jake didn't want to say yes, but the truth was she did look that desperate.

Ashley nodded. "I'll take it." Then she yelled again across the room to Mac, "I'll take it."

Jake stood back and admired her. She might be down on her luck, but Ashley had spunk.

Working at the Rock 'n' Bowl was one adventure after another. Ashley gazed up at what could have been a colorful, abstract, 3-D painting. Blobs of pink, blue, red, and green swirled together. Then she sighed, pulled out her tool, and got to work, scraping the globs of gum from under a table. She was lying on her back, pushing on a tough piece when it broke loose and landed in her mouth.

"Ugh!" She spit out the gum and scrubbed her tongue with napkins.

Mac watched from across the room, plunger in hand.

Next stop — the men's room. But first Ashley put on three layers of rubber gloves.

The last thing she had to do every night was polish the lanes. Wearing her prettiest high heels, Ashley used a huge industrial buffer. Only instead of starting at the pins and working her way backward, Ashley pushed it ahead of her. The next thing she knew, she was slipping and sliding on the newly waxed lanes, landing on her butt as the buffer went haywire.

Max crossed his arms and shook his head in disgust. He hadn't had an employee this bad since Jake first started.

But within a few days, Ashley changed from her Manolo Blahniks into Nikes. She carried a huge tray of food without dropping anything and even remembered to walk around a ladder instead of under it. And a customer even gave Ashley a tip.

Growing more confident, Ashley polished a bowling ball while checking her horoscope in the paper. She put the ball on the shelf, still reading. It knocked against another ball, which knocked yet another. It was like a repeat of the sculptures in Gallery Muse. There was an avalanche of bowling balls. Customers ran in fear.

Ashley threw the paper into the trash. Her luck hadn't turned, and next on Mac's list of chores was spraying disinfectant into bowling shoes.

Jake and the members of McFly hung out at a table.

"Before Phillips will release the album, he wants to see you play in a larger space, like the Knitting

Factory," Jake explained. "See you if you can hold a big crowd for an hour. Create some preheat."

"Where? When?" Tom asked.

"Hey, you guys! Listen!" Mac turned up the radio. They heard the opening notes to "Five Colors in Her Hair."

Tom jumped to his feet. "That's us."

Jake and the band danced around, giving each other high fives.

"How about we celebrate this with a free drink?" Mac asked.

"Brilliant!" Tom said.

"Cool!"

Mac was pouring the sodas. He called out to Ashley, who was leaving the men's room with a plunger and a gas mask. "Hey, Ashley. Scamper up that ladder and change the light." He pointed to a light fixture above the counter.

Ashley peered up at the dark fluorescent tube in the ceiling. From the floor it seemed really far away. "I'm not so good with . . ."

"Thanks," Mac interrupted. He handed her a new tube.

". . . heights," Ashley finished, but Mac was already on his way over to Jake and the guys.

"Phillips will tell us tonight," Jake was saying. "In the meantime we have to focus on fine-tuning a second song . . ."

Tom asked another question, but Jake was distracted by Ashley. He watched her cross under the ladder and then climb slowly and fearfully while carrying the new fluorescent tube.

"See, that's not good," Jake said. "She should've gone up *without* the bulb, and brought down the old one first. Because now when she gets up there she's going to be juggling."

"She's cute," Danny said.

"Yeah," Jake said distractedly. Then, "I mean . . . yeah, she's cute."

Ashley was at the top of the ladder. She tucked the new tube under her armpit and pulled out the old one. She tried to install the new bulb with the old one under her armpit. But she teetered, then tottered. She clutched the light fixture to steady herself and the old tube dropped to the floor and shattered.

"And she should have turned off the light first," Jake said, rising to his feet. "Because now she'll be . . ."

Ashley grabbed the light fixture and got a shock. She screamed.

"Electrocuted," Jake said.

Ashley wobbled again and started to fall.

Jake sprang across the room, vaulted over the counter, and caught her in his arms in one smooth motion.

✳ Chapter Twenty-one

Jake put antiseptic lotion on Ashley's fingers while she held a cold bottle of soda to her head. Her hair stood out in frizzy strands, like an electric lion's mane.

"So, other than, you know, getting zapped, how's the job working out?"

"I can't complain," Ashley said.

"That's good," Jake said.

"No, I mean I'm *literally not allowed* to complain. I had to sign something." Ashley enjoyed the way her fingers felt in Jake's hands, even though he was just applying first aid. "You're very handy with this stuff."

"Thanks." Jake held up his backpack. "It pays to be prepared. I've got everything in here from first aid to extra socks."

"Isn't that being a little defeatist?" Ashley asked.

"It's being a *realist*," Jake said. "You've been out there. Let me see your cell phone."

"Why?" Ashley asked.

He took it from her and scrolled through her contact list. "Bergdorf's? Bendel's department store? *Sushi?* What are you, nuts? You need *hospitals*. Saint Joe's is downtown, but Lenox Hill has a shorter ER wait time. Also never call 911 — they take forever. Firemen respond faster. And when you call the National Poison Control Center, ask for Lou. He's very good."

Jake returned the phone, then checked Ashley's hands again. He held on to them for a moment longer than he really needed to. "You're healing nicely," he said.

"I'll probably just get hurt again," Ashley said.

"That's the attitude!"

Ashley laughed.

Jake picked up his backpack and looked at it like it was an old friend. "I think you need this more than I do."

Ashley hesitated.

"Please," he said.

Ashley nodded, noticing that Jake's warm brown

eyes were absolutely adorable. They eyed each other. Neither one knew what to say. Then Jake's phone rang.

Jake checked his caller ID. "I have to take this," he said.

"Sure," Ashley said, disappointed. Was he about to ask her out?

"Hi, Katy," Jake said into his phone. "How's my girl?"

His girl? "I've got to get back to work," Ashley said, grabbing the backpack. She took one last look over her shoulder as Jake — all smiles — talked to Katy.

Ashley, Maggie, and Dana sat around eating pizza while Maggie's song "Stronger" played in the background.

"The guy actually caught me before I hit the ground and then treated my wounds!" Ashley said.

"Maybe your luck is turning around," Dana said, handing Maggie a slice.

"Uh-uh. He's taken," Ashley said. "Before I forget, here's my part of the rent." She reached into her backpack and handed Dana a big bag of quarters.

Maggie and Dana stopped eating in mid-chew.

"Yeah, I get paid in quarters," Ashley said. "Some tax reason." Before they could object, she changed the subject. "Maggie, that song is so pretty. Is it new?"

"You really like it?"

Ashley took a big bite. "It's awesome. Like the pizza of music."

"Sounds like Ms. Sushi's having a culinary change of heart," Maggie teased.

Ashley held up her slice like she was making a toast. "To complex carbohydrates!"

"To complex carbohydrates," Maggie and Dana said together.

The three best friends made a pizza toast and took three big bites.

✳ Chapter Twenty-two

Jake listened as Harry lay down a drum track.

"The Knitting Factory fell through," Phillips said, joining him.

"Shoot," Jake said.

McFly stopped playing.

"But 'Five Colors' has been getting such good radio play that I decided to book McFly at the new Hard Rock Cafe in Times Square," Phillips said.

Danny and Tom let out a whoop. Dougie broke into a big grin and clapped Jake on the back. Harry drummed his cymbal.

Phillips turned to leave, then stopped. "You pick a follow-up song?"

"We're working on it," Jake said.

"Cool. Get back to work."

"So when do we get to hear this awesome

follow-up?" Danny asked, as soon as Phillips was out of earshot.

"As soon as you write it," Jake said with a worried expression.

"Oh, yeah," Danny said. "That."

The band horsed around for a few minutes, excited about the idea of playing the Hard Rock Cafe.

"Danny, let's work on your vocals for 'Too Close to Comfort' some more. I think we're on the right track," Jake said. He saw Ashley through the glass window and waved her in.

Ashley passed a table full of catered food in the hall and entered the rehearsal room with a carton of takeout from the Rock 'n' Bowl. She carefully placed it on a table as McFly began to play "Too Close to Comfort."

"Here, let me help," Jake said.

Ashley jumped and bumped the lamp with her elbow. She grabbed the lamp to steady it, and tipped the table. Jake dove and managed to save most of the food before it hit the floor.

"Thanks," Ashley said with a nervous smile.

"No problem," Jake said. "Did you hear? We're playing the Hard Rock."

"That's great."

"Yeah, it's just —" Jake checked to make sure the band wouldn't overhear. "There's no way we're going to be able to fill a club that size. I'm dead."

This was Ashley's territory — her old territory, anyway. "It's tough, but not impossible. Get out a press release that says which celebs will be there."

"Celebs?"

"I know some publicists whose clients are into the music scene. I could see if any of them will still take my calls," Ashley said.

"That'd be great. Thanks." Jake gulped. He was definitely lucky these days, but still not experienced in asking girls on dates. "You think maybe we could get a coffee later? I could use some more tips."

"That would be nice," Ashley said. Was he asking her out?

Behind Ashley, Katy waved from the hall.

"Oh!" Jake said. "There she is."

He waved back through the window. Katy, decked out in all new clothes, was putting ketchup on a sandwich by the catered food table. The ketchup package exploded in her face, and she bent down to grab a napkin.

Ashley turned, and got a view of Tiffany at the other end of the table. "Is that Katy?" she asked.

"Yeah," Jake answered.

Ashley's shoulders slumped. Jake wasn't asking her out. He was just asking for help.

"She's sweet, huh? She picked out this coat."

"Looks like a tramp," Ashley said under her breath.

"What?"

"Camp. She looks like someone I went to camp with," Ashley said.

"Okay," Jake said, confused by the sudden sharpness in Ashley's tone.

"I'd better get going. Mac wants me to reset the rat traps."

"So, about tonight . . ."

"You know what?" Ashley said. "I totally forgot. I have other plans. Maybe some other time."

Jake watched her leave, wondering, *What just happened?*

Katy climbed out of Jake's Lincoln Town Car in the rain that evening, across the street from the Rock 'n' Bowl. "I'll see you later," she said.

"Let your grandma know," Jake reminded her. "I'll send the car to pick you up, and don't forget your homework."

"Yeah. Yeah. I hear you."

Katy ran into her building just as Ashley left the Rock 'n' Bowl wearing Jake's old backpack.

Jake watched her start to open her umbrella inside the bowling alley. "No! No! Not inside," he said to himself. "Don't do that."

Ashley hit the street with the umbrella in front of her. It immediately blew inside out and ripped in half. She was drenched in the downpour. After struggling to fix it, Ashley held the broken umbrella up over her head and started down the street, getting soaked. Jake's car pulled up beside her.

"You know there's a poncho in that backpack," he said.

"I didn't even think to look," Ashley answered.

"Can I give you a ride?"

"There's no need," Ashley said. "But thank you. I can walk. I only live, like, twenty-nine blocks from here." She pointed down the block and her keys flew out of her hand, through a subway grate, and on top of a train passing underground. "Oh, no! No!"

"Your keys?"

"Are on their way to Hoboken," Ashley said.

"Do you have a spare in your backpack?" Jake asked.

"That would be *lucky*," Ashley said.

Jake opened the car door. "Hang out at my place until your roommates get back."

"I don't think so," Ashley said.

"I have a satellite TV, a washer-dryer, microwave popcorn. . . ."

Ashley hesitated. Thunder cracked overhead.

Jake could tell that she had changed her mind. "Toss that 'lightning rod' and get in before I get soaked, too."

Ashley smiled, dumped the umbrella, and climbed in.

Neither one of them noticed the bolt of lightning hit Ashley's umbrella as the car pulled into traffic.

✳ Chapter Twenty-three

Jake ushered Ashley into his gorgeous new apartment, courtesy of Downtown Masquerade Records. She took in the place, shivering and soaking wet.

"I'll get you some dry clothes," Jake said. "The laundry room is that way." He pointed. "The bathroom's over there. Go whichever way you think you should go."

A few minutes later, wearing Jake's shorts and a button-down shirt, Ashley watched Jake put her wet clothes and a small scoop of detergent into the washing machine. It was so new and fancy that it had a computerized touch pad.

"Laundry *in* your apartment," Ashley said, referring to the fact that most New Yorkers had to trek to the Laundromat. "As far as I'm concerned, that's when you know you've arrived."

Jake nodded, then sniffed his T-shirt. "Excuse me."

Ashley watched in a mirror as Jake stepped out of the room and took off his shirt. Flustered, she bumped into the washer and knocked over the laundry soap.

Jake popped his head around the corner. "Throw this in for me, will you?" The phone rang. "I'll be right back."

Ashley tossed the shirt into the machine and pushed the button to close the lid. The washing machine locked and began filling with water. It was Ashley's first moment of peace and quiet in days, and she closed her eyes for a moment with a sigh. But the moment didn't last long. Her hand was suddenly covered in bubbles, and more and more bubbles were oozing out of the machine.

"Oh, no." She picked up the box of now-empty laundry detergent and realized what had happened. She tried to open the lid. It was locked.

"Unlock," she cried. "Where's the unlock button?"

Jake called to her from the next room. "Everything okay in there?"

"Fine. Just fine," Ashley lied, trying desperately to open the lid. It wouldn't budge. Bubbles cascaded down the side of the machine, hitting the floor. She punched button after button on the LCD screen. Lots of functions came up, but there was no off or unlock.

"Since when does a washing machine have to be a computer!" she cried. She found the pipes behind the machine and tried to turn a knob. "Water off. Water off," she chanted. The knob wouldn't budge.

Ashley went back to the lid. She pulled on it with all her might. The lock mechanism cracked and the door flew open, hitting her in the face. A torrent of suds surged out of the machine, filling the room.

"Oh, no," Ashley said. She tried again to find an off button but instead the machine went into a crazy-fast spin cycle, spraying bubbles everywhere. In a panic, Ashley slammed the laundry room door.

Jake knocked.

"I'm fine," Ashley said in a high-pitched panic. "No need to come in."

Jake slowly opened the door. The room was filled with suds. Ashley had somehow detached a couple of hoses and they flew around like angry snakes, spewing water and bubbles everywhere.

Jake ran in and hit a button. Instantly the machine stopped and the water stopped flowing. Suds covered everything — including Ashley. She wore a bubble crown on her head.

"What can I say? I'm a pathetic disaster and I, I . . ." Ashley cracked up. "I give up."

"You give up?" Jake laughed.

"Yup." Ashley's stomach hurt from laughing so hard. "I don't care anymore. And it feels great!"

"I know." Jake was laughing, too, now.

Ashley raised an eyebrow. How would he know?

"I gave up years ago. It's my secret to happiness." Jake tried to look worldly and cavalier, but instead he slipped on some bubbles and hit the ground with a splat.

Ashley laughed even harder and threw suds on him.

Jake splashed her back and they got into a crazy suds fight, throwing bubbles at each other until they were both totally covered. Jake grabbed Ashley's hands, and she slipped to the floor. Her eyes got wide. Was he going to kiss her?

"Am I interrupting something?"

Ashley saw a little girl in the doorway.

"Hi, Katy," Jake said.

"*You're* Katy?" Ashley asked.

"Last time I checked."

Maybe my luck is turning, Ashley thought.

Ashley and Katy shared a mushroom-and-pepperoni pizza while Jake talked to Phillips on the phone.

"So Jake tells me you're a loser," Katy said.

Ashley dropped her slice. "Jake said that? I'm not a loser."

"It's cool," Katy said. "I'm a loser, too. It's like a term of affection, not a permanent condition. You just haven't had any good luck is all. . . ."

Jake hung up the phone, clearly frustrated.

"What's the problem?" Ashley asked.

"Phillips wants the new track ready before the concert."

"And?"

"And we don't have one. We have nothing," Jake said.

"Don't stress it," Katy said. "I'll write you a great song."

"Since when are you a songwriter?" Jake asked.

"You could be a little more supportive." Katy pretended to pout.

"Katy. This is serious," Jake said.

"No kidding," Katy answered.

Ashley cleared her throat to get their attention. Katy and Jake stopped bickering and focused on her.

"I think I can help you out," she said.

✳ Chapter Twenty-four

Ashley, Dana, Jake, and McFly listened to Maggie play "Stronger" at the DMR recording studio the next morning.

"If you don't want to use it," Maggie said when she finished, "I totally understand."

"No," Jake answered. "I think it's good. It just needs a few little adjustments to make it seem less girly and alternative." He passed out lyric sheets. "Harry, double the tempo. Danny and Tom, why don't you kick it off tight and rough it up a bit."

The band nodded and left the others behind in the control room as they headed for their instruments.

"Ready. Set. Go," Danny said into the microphone.

*"The world would be a lonely place
without the one that puts a smile
on your face . . ."*

It sounded awesome. The band was having a
great time with the song. Jake gave Maggie a thumbs-
up, and Maggie beamed at Ashley and Dana.

Phillips strode into the room. "I heard a rumor
that you had another hit for me," he said over the
music. "Sounds promising."

Jake practically fell over with relief. "I've got a
good feeling about this one," he said.

"Yes!" Phillips said. "Positive thinking. That's
what I like to hear. And congrats on selling out."

"Selling out?" Jake asked.

"Yeah, I BlackBerried you," Phillips said, pulling
out his own portable wireless e-mail, cell phone,
and organizer.

"I don't have a BlackBerry," Jake said.

Phillips snapped his fingers, and Tiffany made
a note.

"You sold out! The Hard Rock. There's a line of
people just hoping to get in." Phillips grabbed Jake
and pulled him into a bear hug.

Ashley smiled at Maggie.

"I do not hug people. I want you to know that. But, brother, you really saved me twice. Once at the Masquerade Bash and now this."

Ashley leaned forward, suddenly alert. Jake was at the bash?

"It was a good night for me, too," Jake said. "As a matter of fact, since then I've been about *the luckiest guy in the world.*"

Ashley's face lit up as everything became clear.

"Come by my office later, and I'll show you what I'm thinking for the album cover," Phillips said as he left.

"It can't be," Ashley said, stunned, under her breath.

She grabbed Dana and pulled her aside. "It's him," she whispered. "Jake is the guy I kissed at the Masquerade Bash."

"No," Dana said.

Ashley nodded. "Yes!"

"No, really?" Dana asked.

"Yes," Ashley insisted.

"NO!"

"YES!"

"That's great," Dana said. "He's totally cute!"

"No! You don't understand. I kiss Jake again and it's hello, fabulous, carefree life," Ashley said.

"And that's a problem?" Dana's forehead was wrinkled in confusion.

Ashley smiled at her friend and realized it didn't have to be a problem at all. She squared her shoulders, marched up to Jake, put her arms around his neck, and kissed him.

Like the first time they kissed at the Masquerade Bash, the electricity between them crackled. It was a supernatural, tingling-in-their-toes, butterflies-in-their-stomachs kind of kiss. The band started whooping and hollering. Maggie smiled and shook her head.

Jake came up for air. "Ashley," he whispered, then leaned in for another kiss.

Ashley gazed at him, then realized what would happen if they kissed again. "Oh, no!" She pulled away and put her hand over her lips as she backed out of the room. "I need to go now."

"Why?" Jake asked. His forehead crumpled in confusion. "I thought . . ."

"Ashley?" Dana said.

But Ashley was already out the door.

The guys in the band shared a laugh. "You sure know how to pick them, Jakey boy!"

Jake laughed weakly.

Dana caught Maggie's eye and shrugged.

Jake picked up a can of soda and popped the lid.

Fzzzplat!

The can sprayed soda all over him. Jake looked down at his wet shirt and then at the door Ashley had just run through. Something strange was going on.

Ashley slammed the studio door behind her. Could that really be the last time she'd ever kiss Jake? she wondered. Was her luck back? She ran out to the sidewalk.

"Taxi!" she called.

Not one but two taxicabs screeched to a halt in front of her.

She waved them on. "Never mind. I was just checking." Then she pumped her fists in the air in triumph and yelled loud enough for the whole street to hear: "YES! MY LUCK IS BACK!"

She punched her arms again and accidentally hit a man in the face who was running past. He landed on the ground.

"Oh, my gosh! I'm so sorry, sir." *Maybe my luck isn't back,* she thought.

But just then, two cops ran up and grabbed the man and handcuffed him.

"We got him!" the first cop said. "Thanks, miss. Purse snatcher."

Ashley's smile was huge. She started to glide down the street, too preoccupied to notice Peggy Braden.

"Ashley!" Peggy said.

"Ms. Braden. I'm so sor —" Suddenly Ashley noticed who was with Peggy. "Antonio?"

"Hey, Ash," he said sheepishly.

"How lucky we ran into you," Peggy said. "I feel just horrible about those things I said to you. Jail does not bring out the best in people."

"Stop." Ashley held her hand up. "You were right to blame me."

"Well, then let me blame you for bringing this sweet, wonderful man into my life."

Antonio flashed a new diamond band with a big grin. "We're getting married!"

"No way," Ashley said.

"It's true," Peggy said. "I just bought him the ring."

Ashley took Antonio's hand. "That's some rock. Especially for a man."

"We don't get hung up on traditional male-female roles," Antonio explained.

"Well, good for you," Ashley said. "Congratulations."

"I want you to come back and work for me, Ashley," Peggy said.

Ashley's jaw dropped. "You're kidding?"

"I can't lose you. You're my good-luck charm."

"YES!" Ashley shouted, then tried to act calm and cool. "I don't know what to say."

"We have a big pitch tonight." Peggy rummaged through her purse. "Lacoste has a new fragrance, Touch of Red, Fuchsia, some color . . ."

"Touch of Pink, darling," Antonio said.

Peggy pulled a perfume bottle out of her purse and checked the label. "Isn't he a doll?" She handed Ashley the bottle. "Here's a sample to get your creative juices flowing. The St. Regis at eight o'clock. Say you'll be there — by my side."

Peggy held up a platinum credit card and handed it to Ashley. "Wearing something appropriate to your new 'Vice President' title."

"Thank you, Peggy." Ashley stared down at the credit card as Peggy and Antonio strolled off, arm in arm. Her emotions swirled. "Olé, señor," she said.

* Chapter Twenty-five

Maggie and Dana put the finishing touches on their hair and makeup.

"Who wants a late lunch?" Ashley sang from the doorway. She waltzed in dressed in a stunning new outfit, her arms filled with Dolce & Gabbana shopping bags and a big box of sushi.

"Ta-da!" She twirled, modeling her new clothes.

Dana and Maggie silently went back to getting ready.

"Last one in stock and just my size!" Ashley said. "Lucky, huh? Then, I went to Miyakami and bought two orders of everything on the menu. I thought we could have a little celebration."

"That's nice." Maggie tried to smile.

"What's going on?" Ashley asked, finally noticing her friends' slumped shoulders and long faces.

"The band isn't going to do Maggie's song," Dana answered.

"Why not?"

"Phillips is *superstitious,*" Dana said with a sneer.

"He thinks new groups should only perform music they wrote themselves," Maggie said.

"That's crazy," Ashley said.

"It's just bad luck, is what it is," Maggie said quietly.

"You remember bad luck, don't you, Ashley?" Dana said pointedly.

"What's that supposed to mean?" Ashley asked.

"Nothing." Dana glared at her.

"Hey, guys, I'm sorry this is happening, but it has . . ."

Maggie jumped in. "It's not your fault. It's just life." She checked her watch. "Wow, we need to get going. I want to wish the guys luck before the concert."

"You're still going?" Ashley asked.

"VIP tickets," Maggie said. "It would be a shame to waste them." She grabbed her coat. "Aren't you coming?"

"Actually," Ashley said, "I'm not going to be able to make it tonight. I have a . . . meeting."

"Job interview?" Dana asked.

"It's a funny story, but Peggy rehired me," Ashley said.

Maggie tried to be enthusiastic. "That's great. Wow! I'm so proud of you. You stuck it out and everything got better." She gave Ashley a big hug.

"Are you sure you're okay?" Ashley asked.

Maggie shrugged. "What choice do I have? I mean if you sit around making too big a deal about the bad things in life, you miss all the good."

Dana held the door open. "C'mon, Mag. It's getting late."

"Good luck at your meeting, Ash," Maggie called over her shoulder.

Ashley was alone with a platter of sushi. She took a bite and headed to the bathroom to check herself out in the cracked mirror. She caught sight of Jake's backpack and took another long look at her cracked reflection.

She grabbed her coat and charged through the door, only to be stopped by the Publishers' Clearing House Prize Patrol, complete with TV crew, confetti, and oversize check.

"Ashley Albright?" said a gentleman with a TV announcer's voice.

Ashley pushed them aside. "Not now!" she said, and ran off.

Jake and McFly peered out from backstage. The Hard Rock Cafe was filling quickly. The energy and excitement coming from the audience was amazing. Jake had never experienced anything like it.

"Okay, guys," Jake said, trying to keep his own nervous energy out of his voice. "Final touches. Dressing room. Now."

The band filed down the hall while Jake talked to the stage manager. Harry, bringing up the rear, nervously drummed on everything he passed. He threw his drumsticks up into the air like batons and caught them on the way down. Next he added an extra spin. One drumstick flew behind a large rolling "Road Box" and into an open trapdoor.

"Craptastic," Harry muttered. As the rest of the band moved on, he climbed down the hole.

Jake and the stage manager walked past. Jake kicked the open trapdoor closed.

"Someone could fall down that hole," he said.

Harry had just picked up his drumstick when the door slammed shut, leaving him in total darkness. "Hey!" he called. "Hello?"

The stage manager rolled the Road Box over the door as an extra precaution.

*   *   *

Dana and Maggie stood on the corner, trying to hail a cab. Two drove right by. Suddenly, a taxi screeched to a halt and honked its horn. Ashley rolled down the window. "Hey, Maggie! Dana! Get in," she said.

Damon Phillips and his entourage stepped out of his limo and headed into the Hard Rock Cafe. He took in the lights and the crowd around Times Square and smiled when he realized the line snaking down the block were overflow customers who wanted to say they were at McFly's debut concert.

Flyers and graffiti from a thousand other bands filled the dressing room walls. The guys had their guitars strapped on and were getting psyched. Jake entered the dressing room and found Katy hanging out with the guys.

"Katy, what are you doing back here?" he asked.

"Getting to know McFly," she said.

"Yeah, well, you're not old enough to hang out backstage. Besides, you already know these guys."

"Yeah, but now they're going to be famous!" she said.

Jake ushered her to the door. "You. Now. Seat," he said.

He turned to the guys. "Ten minutes. You ready?"

"Born ready."

"Oh, yeah!"

"Stoked!"

There were high fives all around. Dougie played a fast scale to warm up his guitar fingers.

Pop!

"My e-string," Dougie said.

"My eye!" Danny rubbed his eye.

Jake tried to take it all in stride. His bad luck was not coming back. "Now, guys, you've never played a house this big so —"

"Hold that thought," Danny said. Overcome with nerves, he vomited into a trash can.

Tom turned pale and tried to smile, then he did the same.

Jake focused on Dougie, who shrugged and calmly headed toward the stage.

"We might need some air fresheners back here," Danny said, still rubbing his eye. "And by the way, have you seen Harry?"

Jake's eyes got wide.

From the hall, the stage manager called, "Two minutes."

"He's not with you?"

* Chapter Twenty-six

Ashley urged the taxi driver to go faster. Dana and Maggie stared at her as if she had gone totally crazy. What was the emergency?

"Turn left here," Ashley said. "Union Square is always a mess."

"I can't believe you blew off Peggy Braden," Dana said.

"She'll get over it," Ashley said. "If Jake's bad luck is half as bad as mine was, we don't have much time." She pressed her foot down on the floor as if she had a gas pedal. "Step on it, buddy," she urged the driver.

The cab driver stepped on it. The girls were thrown back in their seats. Maggie and Dana eyed each other. Was this their Ashley?

*   *   *

Under the stage, Harry continued to bang on the trapdoor. It wouldn't budge. He could hear the fans screaming for McFly, but no one could hear him.

"Heellooo! Heellpp!"

The search was on. Tom, Danny, Dougie, and Jake raced around backstage, looking for Harry. Tom checked the costume area. Danny looked under every stall door in the men's room. Dougie yelled up into the walkways for the light crew above the stage.

The audience was getting edgy. Jake was checking the stage's wings when Phillips came backstage.

"Jake, my man," Phillips said. "I know you want to keep them waiting, but the natives out there are getting restless."

Jake checked his watch, stalling for time. "Oh," he lied, "we thought it was normal to go on half an hour late."

Just then the guys ran up.

"He's nowhere," Tom said.

"Disappeared," Danny added.

"I've looked everywhere," Dougie said.

Caught, Jake turned to Phillips.

Phillips locked eyes with Jake. "What's going on?"

The girls' cab skidded to a stop. Ashley and Dana rushed to the front doors.

Maggie pointed. "Backstage is this way!"

Harry stumbled through the darkness toward a tiny hole. He could see the audience. There was a series of colored buttons on a control panel in front of him. He pushed one.

Shwooosh!

The area below-stage where Harry was trapped was filled with special-effects smoke. He started to cough.

Backstage, Phillips was in mid-tirade. ". . . and I for one am not looking forward to going out there and telling an angry crowd that the band has decided NOT TO PLAY." He focused on Jake. "Oh, wait. That won't be me. That's going to be you." Phillips was nose to nose with Jake. "Unless you get your guys out there. Now."

"Without a drummer?" Jake asked.

"Impossible," Danny said.

"It won't work," Tom and Dougie added.

A member of the stage crew, his long gray hair in a ponytail, spoke up. "I was the fill-in drummer for Blues Traveler."

"There you go," Phillips said. "A drummer."

"Let me rephrase that," Danny said. "We won't go out there without Harry."

Phillips turned to Jake. "If McFly doesn't play, you'll be lucky to manage high-school marching bands."

Jake heard a commotion behind him and turned to find the girls fighting their way backstage. Ashley marched right up to him, a determined look on her face.

"Ash —"

Before he could finish her name, Ashley grabbed Jake's head and yanked it toward her for a kiss.

Phillips was furious. "What the heck?"

Ashley broke away. Jake was stunned.

"And in five, four, three, two, one . . ." Ashley said under her breath.

*Chapter Twenty-seven

Harry, still coughing, hit the green button in front of him, trying to turn off the smoke. The floor below him started to rise. It was an elevator platform. The audience erupted into applause as Harry rose through the smoke to the center of the stage. He did a mock bow, ran to his drums, and banged on the cymbal.

Tom, Danny, and Dougie yelled backstage. "It's Harry! He's back, and the freak went on without us!"

Ashley smiled at Jake. "Do me one favor? Play Maggie's song."

Jake nodded. "You heard the lady," he said to the guys. "Kick it off with 'Stronger.'"

Phillips glared at Jake, a warning in his eyes.

*   *   *

The guys ran out onstage.

"Ready . . . steady," Tom said.

McFly launched into Maggie's song. Katy danced and cheered in the front row. The band sounded great. The audience loved them.

Maggie stood in the wings next to Ashley, beaming and bouncing up and down. Ashley squeezed her arm.

Phillips leaned over to Jake, who grinned proudly. "Is that the song I told you *not* to play?" he asked.

Jake looked him in the eye. "I guess I'm not superstitious."

Phillips nodded. "If it hadn't worked, I'd have fired you by now. But it works."

The song ended. The crowd went wild.

"I can't breathe. Did people just clap or was that the sound of my nervous system shutting down?" Maggie asked Ashley and Dana.

"They were clapping," Ashley said. "You did it!"

"Thank you, Ash," Maggie said.

Katy sat on Jake's shoulders, while McFly, Phillips, and all his followers celebrated the band's huge success. Jake popped the cork on a bottle of champagne, spraying the entire room in bubbles.

Across the room, Ashley felt something hard hit her on the head. "Ouch!" She bent down and picked up the cork. "Figures," she said to herself.

Maggie came over and gave her a big squeeze. "Hey! What's the matter? You look miserable."

"I've fallen for him," Ashley said, nodding in Jake's direction.

"That's great! What's wrong with that?" Maggie asked.

"For one, the emotions I'm feeling generally lead to kissing," Ashley said with a sigh.

"So?"

Ashley frowned at her.

"Oh, please don't tell me you still believe in all that," Maggie said.

"More than ever. And I can't not kiss him." Ashley reached for her coat.

"Where are you going?"

"Grand Central. I think I'll visit my parents for a while. I need to sort things out." Ashley squeezed Maggie's hand and took one long, last look at Jake from across the room.

Maggie watched Ashley leave, then headed toward Jake.

* Chapter Twenty-eight

Ashley walked into Grand Central Station's almost deserted concourse and checked the Departure/Arrival board. As she approached, all of the slots flipped over to delayed.

Totally defeated, Ashley slumped on a bench. She pulled the pins out of her hair, let it fall around her face, and hung her head.

Suddenly, she heard Jake's voice. "Waiting for the train?"

He stood at the back of the concourse.

"Jake, please."

"Because if you are," Jake said quickly, before she could cut him off, "you might as well give up now. With your luck there will be an announcement that due to a freak switching accident, all trains have been canceled. Then you'll go outside to wait for the bus. At which point the acid rain will start to fall. Perhaps even acid hail."

"I'm sorry, Jake. But I can't see you. It's for your own good."

"Luck changes, Ashley."

"You know?"

Jake nodded. "Everything."

"I swear I'm not crazy. Our luck really got switched. It still is switched." She pulled a lotto scratcher out of her purse. "Here. Scratch one. I dare you not to make money."

Jake wouldn't take it. "So you think meeting me was unlucky?"

"No. I'm happy I met you," Ashley said. "You deserve my luck. You've put it to a lot better use than I ever did."

"Well, I don't want it anymore." Jake moved in for a kiss.

Ashley pushed him away. "Are you crazy?"

"No, I want you to have it."

Ashley ducked.

"It's been great," Jake said. "But I know I'll be just as happy without it."

"How do you know that?" Ashley asked.

"Because." Jake gazed into her eyes. "*You* will be in my life."

Ashley's knees buckled as Jake moved even closer. His lips were practically touching hers when he said, "A few bumps and bruises are a small price to pay."

"No, Jake. I'm, I'm . . ." Ashley fell into his arms and they kissed.

Click!

Click!

Click!

Click!

All of the 'Delayed' slots on the Departure/ Arrival board clicked over to 'On Time.' Ashley and Jake broke their kiss and smiled at each other.

"Tag, you're it," Jake said.

Ashley pulled back an inch or two, and then leaned in again. "You're not getting out of this that easy," she teased, kissing Jake again.

"Oh, yeah?" Now it was Jake's turn to kiss Ashley.

"Not a chance."

They lost count of how many times they had traded the luck back and forth when Katy found them.

"Ugh! Gross! You left me sitting in a limo so you two could kiss?"

Ashley and Jake turned toward her.

"Just my luck," Katy continued. "You take me from a perfectly good party with really cute rock stars, I pop a shoelace, swallow my gum, and how long were you going to leave me out there?"

Ashley's eyes suddenly lit up. "Katy, I'm so glad you're here."

"Why?"

She stepped toward Katy. Katy backed away.

"Why are you looking at me like that?" Katy asked.

Jake understood what Ashley was trying to do. Together, they grabbed Katy and kissed her on opposite cheeks.

"*Mmmmmmm-Ma!*"

"Yuck! I've been slimed." Katy wiped her cheeks.

Ashley handed her the lottery scratcher.

"Cool!"

Katy scratched the card as Jake and Ashley moved in for another kiss. They banged heads.

"Twenty-five bucks!" Katy yelled. "I'm rich. I'm going to take the limo, okay? I have to show this to Grams!" Katy skipped out of the station.

Ashley turned to Jake. "Let's go get a slice of pizza."

"You're on."

They watched Katy jump into the limo and walked down the street, arm in arm.

"Look at that." Jake bent down and picked something up. "A quarter!"

Ashley laughed. "I guess the luck is still with us after all."

They gazed into each other's eyes. In the background, a Con Edison crew jumped out of the way as a burst of water sprayed up from underground. The water shot up into the air as Ashley and Jake leaned in for yet another kiss.

Splash!

Ashley and Jake screamed, then laughed as the water hit them.

Overhead, two shooting stars flew over Manhattan, their glittery trails crossed to form a giant X in the night sky.